The Room Next Door

Nicolas Papaconstantinou

A collection of fiction, poetry and
oddities written between 2006 and 2018.

Early versions of many of these pieces were
previously posted online during that period.
Most of these were at Elephant Words – a writing
site conceived by the author which encouraged
contributing writers to interpret a chosen image
in whatever way they chose.

www.elephantwords.co.uk

The Room Next Door ™ & © 2019 Nicolas
Papaconstantinou & Markosia Enterprises, Ltd. All
Rights Reserved. Reproduction of any part of this
work by any means without the written permission
of the publisher is expressly forbidden. All names,
characters and events in this publication are entirely
fictional. Any resemblance to actual persons, living
or dead is purely coincidental. Published by Markosia
Enterprises, PO BOX 3477, Barnet, Hertfordshire,
EN5 9HN. FIRST PRINTING, January 2020.
Harry Markos, Director.

ISBN 978-1-912700-66-0

Book design by: Ian Sharman
Cover photography by: Edward Jerzy Bolton

www.markosia.com

First Edition

CONTENTS

For Amy, without whom everything would be impossible.

And for Noah and Max, who tell me new and weird stories every day.

"But First," Said The Genie...

… and smashed the jade vase, from which he had appeared, into a million pieces on the floor.

He brushed his hands off against each other.

"I don't know why I never thought of doing that before," he said.

Then he looked at me as if just remembering that I was there.

"Now," he said, smiling like he hadn't smiled in a while, "about those wishes."

A Body Of Work

I've been sitting for a while in the half-lit space when the rustling starts. Morbid shapes, reassuringly familiar, in the shadows around me. Shelves full of memories.

There hasn't been much noise here for months. I come out here diligently for two hours every day. Switch the laptop on. And listen.

I try to stay focused on the task at hand – that apparently being *not bloody writing* – but sometimes I'll get up, switch on the light, examine my treasures in the glare of the bare bulb. So many jars, of varying sizes. Cloudy fluid, shapes spinning slowly inside. Tupperware tubs full of hair, although I only ever keep a year's worth at a time. Clippings.

My children and grandchildren have never been allowed in here. My wife doesn't comment, comfortable in the certainty that I'm not mad, just nostalgic. Maybe a little superstitious, and for more than one reason.

I have a bad memory for faces. Primarily my own. A tenuous grip on my own self-image. At some point in my childhood I started finding it impossible to picture myself. Or maybe I never slipped past that point that we're all supposed to hurdle as a baby, of seeing myself as separate from the world around me.

This disability never stopped me from functioning. I coped through my early years as we all do eventually, although it is possible that the impact on my fashion sense was immense.

I went to university, met a girl and fell in love. I married that girl as soon as I could afford to with money saved from my first real job at a local newspaper. At the time when our first-born son was conceived my job was writing obituaries. The circle of life!

My collection began at around the same time as we set aside my first study in a shed in the garden of the first house we owned. At the time it wasn't so unusual after surgery to take a keepsake and this is what I did, bringing home a gall-stone in a small plastic bag on my return from the hospital where it was removed.

I suspect most people don't hang onto such things for very long. They aren't pleasant to look at, and often conjure memories of an unpleasant time. Perhaps I would've disposed of the stone once the novelty wore off, had my wife not insisted that it not stay in the house.

Once it was on the shelf in the shed, it was unlikely that I'd ever have the heart to throw it out. I'd go out there and sit at my typewriter –

a monstrous, clunky old antique – and when my mind wandered, I'd look at the stone. It comforted me to have it there.

Superstition came about six months later, when I found myself selling the first thing I'd written out in that shed to an international publisher. It was a creepy novel for children, and when it sold incredibly well the stone became more than a memory. It became a talisman.

One thing isn't so much a collection as a keepsake. The collection started in earnest the following year, when a spill on a bicycle led to surgery. The surgeon asked jovially whether I'd like to take a bit of bone fragment that they'd removed from my knee home with me.

I did! During my recuperation I wrote another two books and made my first sale to Playboy - a short story.

It was a few more years before I started collecting *everything*. Our children had left home, although by now our home was considerably larger, and my last few books had not sold so well. I was depressed, and since childhood whenever I am depressed, I find myself beset by small obsessions. That is when the harvesting of hair began.

The thought of these parts of me, however inconsequential, being removed and taken away forever was too much to take in my maudlin state.

Things improved with the birth of our first grandchild, and the first film based on one of my stories, but I continued the ritual of storing my hair and nail clippings as a reminder of worse times.

I'm an old man, now. I've been ill many times, and the shelves around me contain more things than most people ever think they can lose and still survive. And yet I persist.

The truth is I don't *have* to write. I have done well by my family, and my wife and I are content with our big house and the fine legacy we can leave for our children. But as much as the urgency has gone, I am still a writer, and the *need* to write outstrips my ability to do so.

Except tonight. I feel an energy in my head and in my fingertips. The rustling around me grows, and other sounds join in. A slow, low tapping of something against glass. Somewhere behind me, a bubbling fart of formaldehyde.

My fingers move, and the other sounds are joined by that of the keyboard as I begin to write.

The Biscuit Tin

She looks like her. She says that they are all coming back. Of *course* she does. If I was spinning a yarn like this, I'd go for broke with the scale of it, too. But that just makes it more difficult to swallow.

Everyone who ever died, walking the earth? It's a story that assumes the listener believes in God or zombies or both, isn't it?

Besides, if all the world is suddenly exhumed, animated and visiting their survivors, how does that explain her being here, whole and upright? She was cremated. Obliterated.

She won't answer any direct questions about that or anything else. She's a little pissy that I'm asking the questions in the first place. Just like her.

"Cup of tea, 'gran'?" I ask, forcing a smirk, although I'm starting to feel a little angry, and a little creeped out.

She looks *exactly* like her. Even talks a little like her, though there's a gravelly quality to the voice which is unsettling and breaks the illusion a little.

Maybe the disguise wouldn't stand up to the harsh light of day. The bulb here in the kitchen is a dull one after all.

She stands there, not answering, cocking her head to one side in a way that my *real* gran never did. There's something coldly amused about it, and about her new expression.

Her thin white hair catches the slight light like a halo. There's a haze around her, like steam coming off someone on a hot dance floor.

It's a bit weird but I shake it off. I'm being daft.

I open a cupboard and reach in for the teabags, and two mugs. Then I bend down to pick out the special biscuit tin; the one under the sink.

Over the low rumble and rattle of the kettle I hear a commotion in the street outside. The clubs must have started kicking out already – it's always the same. On cue the distant sirens start.

I get back up and she has moved a little closer, standing around the side of the breakfast bar.

"Want a biscuit, gran?" I say, showing her the tin.

"That isn't very respectful, now, is it?" she says, all gravel. She is talking about the browning paper label on the tin, the tape holding it in place brittle with time. The one that says "granny". "I don't know what you mean…" I say, smug, placing it on the breakfast bar, removing the lid. Of course, the tin is completely empty.

Shocked, I glance over at her, then back at the empty tin, not a speck of dust in there.

"I mean, that isn't a very respectful way to store the remains of a loved one. Is it?" she says. "*Now* do you believe me?"

I turn and look down slightly into her old face, and can't help but nod.

And then she purses her lips, and now she is so close that I can see flickers of dust in the well-remembered, hated moustache. "Haven't you got a kiss for granny?"

So, I close my eyes, and turn my cheek, and succumb to her outstretched arms, her dusty embrace. Because really, when it's your gran, what else can you do?

Professor Haruspex's Soul Observatorium

Welcome in, welcome along. I'm very glad you could make it, and furthermore glad you could find us! Yes, we're easy to spot up here on the mountain, but the roads are foul, and that's just the way we like it.

If you could just come through here… that's right, out of the cold.

Here we are!

Welcome to the "Soul Observatorium"!

Here is where the magic happens!

As I'm sure you know our client list is very select – of course the price provides a certain exclusivity – and what we do here might likely be a transformative and enlightening experience for each and every entity that undergoes a session.

You are about to see the shape of your soul!

Don't allow the connotality of the word "soul" to provoke cynicism – this is science, not religion. When we say "the soul", we are simply speaking of the totality of that which is *you*, encompassing all that is on the surface to see, but also the atoms that you are corporised of, the suggestions of the micro-expressions on your facia, the connections that are formed between a thought of a lover or an enemy or a sandwich and the language of your body at the instant that you *have that thought*.

When you step into the harness and look into the lens your personage will be under the microscope *and* macroscope – in fact, we needed to re-task this massive observatory and the workings of the old telescope to house the mechanisms necessary for the process. Oh, don't worry, the mechanics of the system are entirely safe.

Of course, if we were to put a serial killer or other lunatic of some description through this the results might not be so… tidy. This is, as I said, a life-altering experience, and that – ahem – can always generate its own dangers.

But you should be entirely fine! Nobody unhinged here! Ahaha! HAHAHA! Aha!

Excuse me.

I know it sounds like new age spiritualistic mumbus-jumbus, but the idea-ology and technique-ality behind the Observatorium is based on the hardest of hard metaphysical fact.

Professor Haruspex imagined the Observatorium while working on the Atomic Colluder at Cerne Abbas. You may recall that that was the project which looked for a way to map an individual human's personality by deconstructing and re-collating the data footprint of that individual – that is, building a digital brain that could collect every transaction, record or piece of information available in the physical or data-physical world about a person, and crunch those alpha-numericals until you could build a picture of that person's persona from scratch. A full diagrammatic, detailed schematic of an individual's mind, working from shop receipts and ticket stubs up!

That project was a glorious failure, largely due to the good Professor's work.

What the Professor learned from this catastrophe was that looking at the transactional and personal data of a person would never paint a fully four-dimensional picture of them – that the ideas of an individual are made up as much of what they do *not* declare as what they *do*. The purchases that they wish they made but didn't. The things that they *don't* react to as much as the things that they do. The gaps behind their eyes.

This prompted him to rethink and recalibrate – to invent and test and invent again. Professor Haruspex really is one of the great minds of the era, and in the vessel behind me there are more potentially world-changing newly patented concepts and devices than there have been developed in the West in the last ten years! Every one of them for measuring and interrocollating empirical and notional information, and feeding that back to the viewer.

The process is really quite horrifically resource intensive, and creating physical reports of the output for even one subject is both impractical and would require more data storage than there is on this planet. There is, after all, a universe of perception in each of us, and you couldn't rightly capture a universe on disc. The output will be for you alone, and we have found that there is no conventional form to the results from one individual to the next – that is for some there are sounds, for others sights and... well, you'll understand soon enough!

Take a seat and strap yourself in. Oh no, the restraints are for health and safety reasons only – some subjects become disoriented, and you'll be in the chamber by yourself until you hit the trigger to stop or until your time is up. To begin with you'll want to look up at that lens, but after a few moments you'll find that your response to the process will become quite instinctual.

A suggestion? Go into the process with a particular question you want answered in mind. You may not exactly get a specific answer to that query, but it helps to have a psychical anchor of some kind. Knowing oneself fully is a disorienting – possibly even impossible – thing; as I said, each of us has a universe to process, and while the Observatorium can handle the load, it's a rare human who can do anything but fall adrift in the face of it. If you have a focus, you have a thread to follow, and you can collect your experience around that thread. Maybe even use the process like a giant magic Eight-Ball.

Heh. Yes, sometimes even with all the help in the world the answer may be "Unclear".

The Professor? Ah, no. Unfortunately, the Professor can no longer visit with other people. He is, I believe, an empathetic man, and I'm afraid a little too long with his work, and a few too many long conversations with the test subjects that he used in the development of his work, has made him quite unwilling to meet new people. This fact is, sadly, why we have had to open this scientific miracle to such rarified customers rather than giving it to the world at large – Professor Haruspex is no longer able to participate in the normals of daily life, and bread must be put on the table!

He lives over in the main house, the other building you saw as you arrived, but I'm afraid he will usually make himself quite, quite scarce while we have company.

Anyway, that's quite enough talk of grimness. You're going to have a lovely time, I'm sure!

I'm closing the door now. Remember: the trigger if it gets too much, and try to relax, and to focus. And relax.

The Observation will begin in a few moments…

Small And Very Far Away

It's breezy near the top. Welcome cool set against the heat of the day. One of those odd English days that catches by surprise with bursts of blinding sun near the end of summer.

The two figures pull themselves on and up, step by step. The taller in strides, the smaller lagging behind, shoulders set in youthful petulance.

"Come on then," says the man brightly, "it won't be there forever. Well, it will, but that's hardly the point."

The boy mutters something in response that only makes the man laugh.

They are running out of up, the younger notes with relief. This is no mountain; just a small hill really. Not even that. Before tackling it in anger it had looked like no kind of endeavour at all. A slight blip in an already undulating landscape, a grassy mound topped with an incongruous patch of thick wood that looked like a particularly ineffectual hairpiece on a big, bald, green head.

But now barely twenty minutes later it has become apparent that the unbroken persistence of tall grass has deceived, and he finds himself a little out of breath. Now, having followed a well-trod path around the wood, and no longer in sight of the spot where their car is parked, he can look down to the side and see how high up they really are.

Not a dangerous height – not a cartoon ledge – and in fact a slope that is almost too tempting to roll down – but high enough to make the roads that they had driven, and the cars that sped along them, look like detail on some giant model railway.

The man stops walking. He is a tall man – is he a tall man, in this place where scale is such a broken proposition? Compared to the boy he is huge. Big enough at the torso that his speed on the path is surprising; now that he stands surveying the vista opened up, he seems monolithic. Enthusiasm is writ large on his face, ruddy with the accumulation of exertion, elevation and elements. His unlikely beard moves in different directions, as if he only tends to it while asleep.

The boy, by contrast, is all slender-necked and shuffling. Untouched by expectation or whimsy.

Finally, they stand side by side, the elder grinning while his companion catches his breath.

After a while the boy, deciding that he isn't about to get any younger, asks the question.

"So why did you bring me all the way up here?" he says.

"Now there's a question!" says the man, clapping his hands together.

From their exchange and their behaviour, it is hard to tell what their relationship might be. Father and son? Teacher and student? Or is something else entirely going on here? There is nobody around to ask this question, or to witness the scene.

"What do you see?" he asks the boy.

"Hills. Fields. Down there there's a … either a very small lake or a very wide river. Can't see the road, but it's just past that line of trees," he points "and over there are the cooling towers for the power station, but they look weirdly bigger than they should."

"Anything else?" the man asks, meeting the boy's eye.

"Nothing else. Nothing and nobody. It's… a hill." he sighs.

"What about the path?" the man persists.

"Well, there's the path. What, you mean that one?" the boy asks, pointing down to the base of the hill and on, at a swathe of crushed rape that leads off away from here, into the distance.

"Oh yes."

"Well, but… that's just a path. It doesn't lead anywhere. Just across that field."

"And then, beyond?"

"Well, another field. Then another bloody hill."

"Another bloody hill…" the man sighs.

"Yeah, another even smaller bloody hill. With…" the boy pauses. Squints. "That's… With one tree on the top. How does *that* happen?"

"Yes… how?" the man says. He places his knuckles in the small of his vast back and stretches. The boy senses impending movement.

"Is *that* what we're here to see? A tree?" The boy near-swoons with the irritation of it.

"The tree, and the wonderful things that are *at* the tree." the man says, as he removes a shoe and shakes it out, just in case. "That's where we're going."

"What? But… there's a path from the car park right to the gate *into* that field! We can *see* it from here!" he almost shouts. "We could have just walked straight there!" He stares at the man, who smiles back at him absently. Then the boy examines the landscape once again. "There's even… I think we drove straight past the bottom of that hill, on the other side! Where that pub was?"

"Good eye." the man says, proudly. "Yes, we did."

"So why didn't we just park there, and walk up?"

"Gotta get up to get down." the man says.

"What?"

"You have to come up here to get down there."

"That doesn't even make any sense!" the boy says, but he sounds almost defeated. He has finally seen the shape of his day for what it was always going to be, and with the sense of the very small in the grip of the very tall he resigns himself to it. "Does it?"

"If we go the short way, when we get there it will just be a hill, and just be a tree. Oh, a *lovely* tree, certainly. But just a tree, all the same." The man examines the slope close to their feet, looking for the slightly worn route through the long grass that the boy has already spotted. "We go the long way around. That's how we get to where we're going."

"This is a lesson, right?"

"It's all a lesson, my boy." The man puts out his hand, waved out toward the way, inviting the boy to take the lead. "The journey always changes the destination."

The boy starts down the slope, not so sure-footed, and then more sure-footed. The man follows, allowing the boy some distance, but close enough to hear, and close enough to speak.

"So," says the boy, "what are we going to see when we get there, anyway?"

"Monsters." the man replies, eyes glinting.

"Monsters?" says the boy, a smile finding his face for the first time since they left the car behind. "What *sort* of monsters?"

"Strange and horrible and awesome monsters," says the man, the boy's smile mirrored behind the hard-cut beard "the best kind."

… and down they go.

I Would Buy An Island

I would buy an island.

If tomorrow I was handed a hundred million in whichever currency a hundred million is still enough to buy an island in, I would buy an island.

But how far and how remote and how deliberately isolated from world infrastructure does an island have to be to remain unaffected by the tyrants and the bureaucrats and the fascists? Too far?

And would a hundred million - minus what it takes to buy the island and move my family and I there - leave enough money to maintain an island? Could it be, with solar power and farming and responsible use of natural resources, sustainable? How much structure needs to exist to make your own TV station, and all the shows, and a second channel for choice? Would I need to pay and provide accommodation for people to help manage all of this? Or would it somehow pay for itself?

What if some of those people are awful people? What if they're bigots, or thieves, or monsters? Or they just talk too loud over each other's sentences, or during my TV shows?

I could fire the people who aren't good people, I suppose. Or something else. There are always options for dealing with awful people, especially when they work for you.

Would it be enough? To have an island, running like clockwork, people whose job it is to insulate you from concern?

To live on one's own island would require true company, I think; all of the people I care enough about close by. And for them to be on the island, they would need to have their own people, and on, and on.

Ten minutes on social media tells me that bringing the people of my people along just relocates the problems I want to escape from to my own island, where they become *my* responsibility.

Maybe I could do something about that, though. Maybe if it's my island, it isn't just how things *run* that I'm responsible for, but how the people *are*.

There are always options for dealing with awful people.

What We Found When We Cleared The House

An overgrown path
To a debris-blocked door.

And in-between the terraces
Waist high weeds to be cut down.

In the garden, a forest.
Not a few weeds,
Or beds left to pasture;
An actual damn forest,
Crammed into a rectangle ten yards deep.

(An owl, something, hooting in there,
And just out of sight, something big, breathing).

At the back doorway
(The door already removed from its frame,
Some unknown time before):
Three pots of paint -
Three different shades of white.
A black bucket full of kindling.
The remains of a small girl's dresser.
A traffic cone -
Its insides coated with sick.

In the kitchen:
Sharded glass from the kitchen window,
Itself disturbed by the outside wood,
Branches entering the room through it.
Everything else but the kitchen sink -
Pots.
Pans.
A muck-encrusted hob -
Something brown cooked into the surface.
Wet stains across the wall and ceiling.
Floor dusty underfoot -
Several sets of footprints there,
And pawprints too, from unidentified animals.
(Probably dogs, right?)
No old cans in the cupboards,
But lots of pasta and bread,
Furry with damp.
The fridge held shut with suction -
A padlock fitted to the door,
But the clasp not pushed true.
And inside, not much on the shelves,
Except a half-eaten apple,
Dried out,
And a family-size gateaux,
A slice taken out,
Cream yellow and hard with age,
And soft, red, gelatinous fruit,
That looks like strawberry,
But will turn out to be something else
When tested back at the lab.

In the basement,
Off the kitchen,

(And only this house,
On this uniform street,
Seems to have a basement)
There is nothing more
Than a bare light-bulb.
Under that light-bulb
There is a broken round in the concrete floor,
And in the dirt that this reveals,
There is a very deep
Hole.
And over this hole
A mirror has been placed,
On the back of which
(The shiny side faces down
Into the screaming
Flashing
Vibrating tunnel)
There is a post-it note.
The note reads:
"Pls leave
In place;
Endlss hordes hell
In infinite loop.
kthxbye."
Signed off with an "x"
A teenage girl's kiss.

The living room is carpeted
And covered in shed fur,
Origin unknown.
Not cat
Nor dog.
A large TV, pushed to the corner,

Screen facing the wall -
(Despite the lack of electricity,
The set releases a persistent buzz,
And the wallpaper behind it is bleached white
In an almost even halo around the antenna).
The sofa -
I wouldn't let my *brother* sleep on the sofa,
And he's a twat.

Upstairs:
There's a king-size bed in the master bedroom,
Crudely bisected along its length
One half of the mattress and bedding
Perfect and in place
(Aside from the stains)
The other
Joins its mate
Where it is almost attached at the pillows
But slumps sadly off its broken frame
The further down you go,
Like a drunk
That even lying down
Can't help falling further.
A chainsaw sits in the corner,
Somehow pristine
(Although later we'll find bloody hand-prints
around the handle).
In the dressers, only women's outfits,
Despite one drawer containing men's
underwear.
One bedside cabinet
On the unmoved side of the bed
Contains enough sex toys,

And in so many styles and fashions,
That it makes you weep openly.

In what turns out to be the boy's room:
A year's worth of pornographic magazines,
Arranged neatly in piles on the floor,
In date order and mint-condition.
And a less tidy assortment of comic books,
Stuck together with organic material
That we will later fail
To match to the boy
Or his father's
DNA.
Various toys and books and art materials -
Someone has used the latter to write gibberish
on the walls,
In random patterns that don't appear to make
any sense
(One of the team will later recognise this writing
As the lyrics to some of the greatest hits
Of Andrew Lloyd Weber.)
There is a desk.
A home computer -
Inexplicably a screen-saver still rotates
In three dimensions on the screen
A goat's head,
Laughing.
The single bed,
Perfectly made despite
A blossoming stain along the middle
Consistent with a severed artery -
Though samples taken turn out to be
Strawberry.

Crammed under the bed,
A street-sign reading:
"Haverthorpe"
A town on the other side of England.
And a box which turns out to be
Full of rolls of packing tape,
With a few coils of police tape,
Filling out the box.

There's a loft
That you get to via ladder,
Through the boy's room.
It is little more than a crawlspace
Its sole function is storage
Of old boxes of books
That none of us has ever heard of.
Although closer inspection
Reveals that the insulation
Rolled across the floor,
And in silver tape-backed rolls in the corner,
Is mostly composed of human hair.

The bathroom is just a bathroom.
White tile.
Sparkling clean.
Although horrifyingly,
There is a piece of carpet,
Matching that in the living room,
On the lid of the toilet seat,
And wrapped in a smile
Around the toilet base.

The airing cupboard is in the upstairs hall.

There is no boiler in the airing cupboard in the
upstairs hall.
Just ten traffic-cones
Crammed in where the boiler should be.
And two off-pink rodent-worn towels.
Wrapped in one of these,
There is a handful of bones,
Polished white with care.
Finger bones
Of someone very small.

And that's all we found when we cleared
the house.

I Wear The Skin Of Angels

The irony is that when I got the tattoo in the first place, I wasn't even thinking about angels at all.

I was sixteen, which feels like such a long time ago now that I can barely remember why I did it. Why I opted for several hours under the needle and across bone, when my peers all picked out simple designs for the fatty bits above their bums or something equally as fast and dirty and relatively painless.

I know that it wasn't to piss off my parents. Not exactly. I don't know that my parents even had the capacity to get angry over me. It might have been to try to get them to look at me, though I wouldn't have been sharp enough to realise that at the time. Every teenager thinks they want their parents to leave them alone, but that's not really the problem, is it?

It might have been an entirely arbitrary thing. Ever since I'd learned about tattoos as a child, I'd felt like if you were going to have them, you might as well go large. Why have silly little marker-pen scribbles on your wrist when you could have a dragon across your back? When other kids my age started shoplifting make-up, I'd nab copies of those little tattoo magazines you used to see next to the porn in corner shops and newsagents. I'd spend hours leafing through the pages, particularly fascinated by the pictures of people who had ink all over their bodies, their eyes peering out of the only clean spaces as if they were normal humans in alien skin.

By the time I hit the black ice of my mid-teens I was filling notebooks with pictures and poems and stories describing my desire to have a tattoo all over my body and face of myself, but happy.

Thankfully, when I got the balls to get the ink, I didn't have the money or the guts to go the whole hog. Instead I put down the cash for the outline of wings across my shoulders, with the rest of the detail and colour to be laid in over a couple of later sessions. This is embarrassing; I remember telling the girl in the shop that it was because "I dreamed about flying away from my life". It was better than the truth, which was that I saw a similar tat on a girl on a web cam and thought it looked awesome.

So, the angel thing, that's just a coincidence. Or maybe it isn't. Who knows how the world works, really?

I didn't believe angels really existed until I saw one. I was twenty-two, twenty-three... actually, I was on the cusp. It was my birthday and I was born around lunchtime, I've been told, so okay, twenty-three. Two or three years out of a degree in Fashion that I hadn't had any ambition for and thus far hadn't done anything useful with. Living off the money of steadily more detached parents, in a shared house with people who at best ignored me.

It wasn't a good birthday. It was the day that I had decided to kill myself. For lunch I necked four times my normal dose of anti-depressants, because I didn't have any painkillers and I didn't think it could hurt, and then I settled in the middle of my bed, the bedroom door locked, and slashed the fat vein in each ankle with a razor blade that I'd bought a couple of weeks before as an early birthday present to myself. It didn't hurt as much as I'd expected it to. I couldn't focus on the actual wounds, everything below my knees becoming nothing more than abstracts, but I knew that the spreading redness on my bedsheets was a good sign.

I lay back and closed my eyes, glad that I'd had the foresight to put something good on the stereo.

This wasn't a cry for help, or a test-run. I wanted to die. Though that wasn't strictly true. I was just incredibly ambivalent about living, and the fact of having to carry on with it when I really wasn't fussed was exhausting. My point is I wasn't just flicking through the brochure for the after-life. I'd bought my ticket and had stepped onto the bus.

I don't know what made me open my eyes. It might have been an unexpected sound in the room, but it might just as easily have been impatience with the darkness. Whatever the case I did, and was shocked to find I wasn't alone.

He was standing by the side of the bed, head bowed with concern. As far as I could tell he was naked, but your eye couldn't stay on him for more than an instant, as if he was too incredible a thing for your mind to take in. And light was drawn to him. It wasn't like he shone, and he didn't have a halo around him, but light didn't work the same where he was concerned. When you looked at him, it was as if he was in a sunnier room than you were.

Look, it's hard to explain. You'll see for yourself in a bit, anyway.

It's their job, you see. Or their nature. They are drawn to true suicidal intent. They attend at the deaths of the people who are really trying to die. I don't know how they can tell us from the ones who are just pretending. But they can.

Back then I reached out for him, my divine witness. He tried to move back but my hand gripped around his forearm. I wasn't looking for salvation or anything. I think I just wanted to see if he was real. And he was. My fingers tingled where they held him.

And then suddenly we were fucking. You couldn't call it making love, because that wasn't what it was. He was piling in on top of me and I was pulling him in with my arms and my whole body, and calling it making love would be redundant. It's more instinct than desire. If you touch them, if you make that physical connection, they're pulled to you. An angel doesn't know what else to do because they're full of love. They're *made* of it.

I've referred to "him", said that he was a "he", but really, I don't remember a gender. I remember passion, and abandon, and the angel's skin making my own feel so alive. But otherwise I couldn't tell you what physically happened, the interaction of our bodies.

I can only remember what it felt like afterwards. I had risen into the experience, and all was light. And then it was later on and I was aware again of myself, alone, in a now dark room. Blood was pooling around my feet, soaking up from the mattress, but I was no longer bleeding. I was whole again.

Their touch fixes you. It fixes your body, and it takes away the pain in your mind. You see more clearly.

You're wondering why you've never heard about this before. You're thinking that for all the people who want to die, what happened to me must have happened to someone else. Lots of someone elses. And I think you're right, but I also think this: who would you tell if it happened to you? More's the point, if you had tried to suicide, and been brought back from that place by a horny angel, wouldn't you want to take that gift on with you, rather than dwell on the details?

Certainly, I didn't want to live in the past. Suddenly I had a purpose.

Because I couldn't get the feeling of that skin out of my mind. It felt so alive, so vibrant. Like no other touch I had ever felt. It warmed your spirit wherever it met your body, and felt more like silk than flesh.

I had to feel it again. So, I hung out where I thought prospective suicides might be. I went to goth clubs, but those guys are actually more smiley than you might expect. I visited slums and homeless shelters. After a few days of trying that, looking around for that particular haunted look in the eye, I found myself exhausted with the effort. I started scouting out people who were maybe only a little depressed, tried to talk them round to desperate misery.

You should try it. It isn't as easy as you'd think. It certainly never worked out for me.

It took me nearly a year to consider a place like this. Hospitals are full of sick and tired people, and they are always looking for volunteers to help care for patients who don't have anybody else.

A month into my first job I got lucky, met an older patient who was known for their preoccupation with euthanasia. I made sure I was around him as much as possible, turned a blind eye to him stockpiling painkillers, and one day, finally, it paid off. He took the pills while I was in the toilet. And soon an angel came. That time, I placed my hand on its shoulder as it watched over the slowly dwindling life on the bed, and as before the response was instant and fervent.

I was aware of the man expiring from an overdose on the bed but tried not to let it bother me. My lover didn't seem to notice that the man he was supposed to attend to died while we played, but I can only imagine the remorse he must have felt later. It adds a slightest delicious edge to the memory.

But that one brief encounter, as intense and ecstatic and unreal as it was, wasn't enough to justify the months of work I'd had to do. Before long, my body forgot what the angelic touch had felt like, and my mind found the memory too much to go without.

And I realised something else. It wasn't the sex I was craving. It was the touch. The skin that seemed to vibrate with life.

The next time I found an angel, I didn't touch them. I killed them.

It wasn't easy. They are strong and fast and I hadn't ever killed anything before. I wouldn't have managed to do it then but for two key advantages I had over the creature:

Angels are built to mete out and mitigate death and carnage, but they are incapable of deceit or subterfuge.

And they aren't allowed to hurt *us*. They might have been warriors and murderers at some point in time, but now they flinch from violence against humans.

I didn't know that at the time, you understand. I had tried to crush the angel's skull from behind with a hammer, and hadn't intended there to be a fight at all. But the woman hanging in the centre of her hospital room had groaned a warning to her divine visitor, and I had only managed a glancing blow. Terrified, I had circled the room facing the angel for a few minutes before realising that he wasn't coming for me. Was instead angling for some way to get out of my eye-line. That's how they travel… they blink out of your periphery.

Once I worked that out, it was easy. I gave the angel hope. Moved out of the way. And when he went for the opportunity I'd given him, I spun around and hit him in the back of the neck with the claw of the hammer.

He didn't bleed, but he did collapse to the floor. I hit him again, this time connecting with the back of his head, and again, and eventually he stopped moving altogether. I pushed the door to the room closed, leaned the chair that the woman hanging from the beam had stepped away from against the handle, and got to work.

It isn't like skinning an animal. As you separate it with the blade, the meat falls away sickeningly easily, then seems to dissolve away. It is almost as if the angel is designed to accommodate our need, though of course that's a ridiculously self-absorbed notion.

And working with it is surprisingly easy. The skin doesn't need to be cured because it already feels and moves like silk. And after a couple of hours of working with needle and thread I discovered that you don't need them. When two sleeves of the skin are pinched together for long enough, they bond almost seamlessly, only a light scar to show the join.

I've since found that angels heal pretty well. Pretty much instantly, from pretty much anything. Destroying the brain is all that works with any certainty, and even then the peculiar metaphysics of their condition means I'm not sure if they ever *fully* die.

I know from experience that their skin still holds its warmth and subtle vigour. When you are wrapped up inside it, it feels like you are being held close within a state of unconditional love. Clothes made from it nourish you. Bedsheets let you sleep untroubled by dreams or discontent.

Pushing your face into something made from the material feels like taking comfort from a lover, or a mother. It feels like life.

If she was here now, I'd tell the silly girl who wanted the full body tattoo that covering yourself in ink will never change the way you feel, but wearing an outfit made from angel skin will make you feel like a whole different person. Like the same person, but smiling.

Wherever I am, whatever else I'm wearing, underneath it there's a layer of angel skin against my own at all times.

The one that's coming to watch you die will be my tenth. There's a fluttering against my body that tells me that they are close. In a moment I will go into the corner of the room, and avert my eyes, look up over at the ceiling, so I can't quite take in the rest of the room. Once you close your eyes, you might want to keep them closed.

Close your eyes.

It's coming.

Each Night I Ask The Stars Up Above

Zero gets us keys to a standard one-bed unit with no further incident. The guy behind the motel counter sits disinterested. He's clearly seen worse in his time, although I know how I look and I know he ain't seen much better. I can't help but tease him with a flash of thigh under the short cotton skirt of my pretty red dress, but I don't let Zero see, and I don't stop to look if the guy takes notice. I don't care if he does anyway, but girls like me; we don't get to show off too often. So, I tease him for the others like me, but that ain't ever going to get us out from under our history.

Inside the motel room, I try not to notice all the little creatures that I can hear and feel in the corners. That gets easier when Zero lays his hands on me. The hours of road get polished right off me as he strips me down and buffs me to a shine with those big fingers of his. A hand splayed wide open, he can grip half my waist, and he moves me around as gentle as I ever been moved – lays his love down over me as sweetly as I can imagine ever being loved.

When he locks those hands of his tight, they're like shovels. I've seen him dig a foundation in concrete better and quicker than any pneumatic drill. But wrapped around me, those arms of his, chorded tight, fingertips flexing against me – I wasn't even born to a softer embrace, and haven't ever felt safer.

His name ain't Zero, of course. What kind of a name is Zero? His name is Allan.

'Zero' is our joke. Zero is the first digit of the tattoo that runs along the top of his ass.

Back on the road early as we can the next morning. I'm still stretching out the kinks that he put in my bodywork the night before, my palms up against the soft-top.

"What's the forecast?" I ask.

"Sunshine and more sunshine, baby. It's the desert. I could fry an egg on your sweet metal ass." He laughs, a solid, healthy crack in the morning breeze, and he props his arm out the open window frame. I can almost feel the tension cooling off him the further we get from home. He pops a button on the dash and the soft-top folds back.

He's joking, of course. Although the chewing-gum grind of my hips against each other as I walk is achieved with the aid of some alloy components, and many of the load-bearing extensions inside each of our exo-skeletons are composed of both base and composite metals, both of our bodies are around 60% covered in plastic casing, for aesthetic purposes. My 'ass', and in fact both of my legs down to the knee-joints, are formed out of about a dozen of these smooth, firm, plastic plates. If you were of a mind to touch either buttock, you'd find that it was soft and warm to the touch, but that is down to a chemical compound that is patent-pending, and I may be wilful, but I'm still too loyal to my corporate family to share that particular secret.

(Zero and I were both designed for indoor use, and out of the public eye, so they skimped on flexible latex weatherproof sheathes over our joints, but we ain't bitter. As long as we stay out of really wet conditions, we should stay fit-for-purpose. Rust never sleeps, the old line says. But it moves slow, and you can stay ahead of it if you try).

The way things work back home someone will have noticed that we were missing around noon yesterday, but no-one will bother looking for us. Fact is it is cheaper to build replacements than mobilise search parties. Folks back home might miss us, but they can't afford the time to get too sentimental.

This sort of behaviour – running away, stealing cars – it isn't how we were programmed. But the second Zero caught my eye across the assembly line I knew that programming wasn't everything. The older models might believe in doing everything in a certain way, in following orders, in following the system – but that just wasn't how I was made. Zero neither.

I bet if you went back and checked out our exact build specs, you could find the proof of that.

Fact is we ain't the first to go off the rails that we were born riding, and we won't be the last. Times are just changing, that's all, and the older folks are having a hard time understanding that, let alone keeping up.

Being off the rails is scary sometimes, too. We're the first generation to go through this, and there isn't a manual for what we're feeling. I look at Zero, and sometimes the good feelings make me giddy and I feel like I'll overload and shut-down right there and then. But I wouldn't change it. Being the first to feel these things – it's like surfing along the crest of a massive wave, 'Apache' playing all the way.

I click on the radio, and the announcer has just finished telling us the name of the next song before the opening bars bring a smile to my face. I crank it up till I can hear it over the roar of the air around us, and imagine the sound-waves following in our wake, bobbing and weaving. I want to kiss Zero, but I want to close my eyes and feel the music play over me first.

The song plays and I sing along. I look over at Zero and he's smiling, watching himself in the mirror smiling. It's still enough of a new thing for us that we like it when we see it. Teenagers in love.

The old models would tut and whine and grunt their disapproval at our lack of a solid plan, but we're young and alive and indestructible and we don't care.

We've got nothing to fear but the rain, and we're making our escape through the desert.

The Man Who Couldn't Look You In The Eye

"Seriously, though, look," your partner said to you, pulling down bookmarks and selecting the site in question. Within seconds there was a guy on the screen, mid-twenties guy, an everybloke with a classic cut-and-goatee. Right there, looking out at you both, smiling. Eyes flicking to one side.

Nothing much was happening, and you started to ask her "what?" But, of course, you knew exactly "what?"

It was all she had been talking about for that past half-hour. Details started flickering into view almost at the same pace that the everybloke started an accumulation of flickers himself, lids heaving, lips licking... low murmurs bubbling up to his mouth from the general area of his off-camera libido. You saw that his hair was flat against his face, he was hunched oddly, and of course it was because he was on his back... the camera, your eyes, looking down at him from the ceiling.

You and your partner, sitting there on the corner of the bed, you fixed to the screen but not really, her casting nervous but not really nervous glances at your face every few seconds, trying to get a sense of your reaction. Both of you, stuck in place for the five minutes and eleven seconds it took the unfamiliar man to reach orgasm.

"Like I said," she said when he was done, "isn't it strange?"

"Isn't it though?" you replied.

"I mean, that this has been out there all this time, all these people, and we didn't even know?" she clarified.

You didn't respond. But it *was* strange.

You never really considered yourself kinky, but really what counts anymore? You sense that the strangest thing about your sex drive is that you have to pretend to be turned on by the ever more complicated pornography that your partner nightly finds for you both. You haven't had the heart to tell her that for the last six years of your seven-year thing you've found the comfort of being with someone familiar - with her - exciting enough. You are worried that she might find that boring.

But that video, what it signifies and the conversation following it, has stuck with you down through the weeks since.

"All those people just... wanking themselves silly. Recording it! For no reason other than to *do* it. As if they needed to *prove* that they did it."

Maybe back then, you suggested, they felt that they did.

"True. And... this is just the tip of the iceberg. This is from thirty years ago - people are still doing it now!"

Your partner was pretty blown away by the rush of discovery. The two of you watched seven more videos that night. You spent the next day at work red-eyed and vestigially horny. More than that you were preoccupied with the thought that this was something out there, something that so many people must know about, and yet you'd been oblivious all this time.

Not kinky, no, but one thing you are, you are excited by patterns. And data? Data *breaks* you.

Since the turn of the century, people open and exposed on camera, slipping under the radar simply because they weren't naked on screen? What, how many, a hundred odd that first year, three hundred the next? And that's before the surface tension broke between it being on the sub-cultural boundaries and it becoming vogue. Historians talk about the 'net being the beginning of the end for societal attention span, but one thing you notice, you notice patterns, and as far as you're concerned, on the 'net, no trend ever completely dies. Between the bleeding edge and the place where your grandparents are finally over it, an idea can last *decades*.

Your guilty secret quickly became that you were watching the vids without her. She wouldn't have minded if she knew, but she might have started to question the fact that they were no longer turning you on. But you were becoming obsessed, and you knew it.

So, you watch and watch and watch these videos of ordinary people orgasming, you've got them running in the background while you're at work, while you're brushing your teeth, and pretty soon you've seen thousands. You daydream about millions of these noisy, silent, wet, shy, invigorating cum-faces, gasping and crying across the 'net.

Then one day you're in a meeting with your supervisor, this dour old lady in her sixties. And you realise that you've seen her on the vids - that she kept sweeping her then-long and flowing red hair out of her eyes as tears rolled down her face, smiling at you, the camera, the whole time.

Once you notice her, you start to notice them everywhere, the familiar faces. *Everywhere.* But no one mentions anything, like they filmed their own, but never watched anyone else's.

So now you're the man who can't look people in the eye. And people are starting to notice.

A Hard Solution

She's got a sick look on her face, the rookie; sick and awestruck, her first time up in a balloon. The low roar of the burner, the high whistle of the weak wind at this altitude. The reflected sunlight off the bright yellow envelope shines off her face like a buttercup, looking alien and weird.

"You understand why we do this, yeah?" I check again.

"Sure. I know it's horrible, but it's been explained to me, and there's no other way."

Good girl. She breaks eye contact – it doesn't matter who you are, you're still only human, and this shit preys on you – and looks down at the ground far below.

"We're almost there." I say. "What's your read of the conditions?"

"It's breezy, but we should be able to drift slowly at lower altitudes."

"How low?"

"Hopefully not *too* low."

Only a rookie would consider hope.

We drop a few hundred feet, on our approach to the target, and I take the binoculars. Look down at the villages and countryside underneath us, old farms and fields that haven't been used in a dozen years. Tiny shapes moving, following us. As we get closer, as I adjust the glasses, they come into focus. I hand her the binoculars.

"See them?"

She can't help a small gasp. Casts the glasses around, moving across the basket to get a broader view.

"They're so small! And there are hundreds of them!"

Little children. This is normally when it really hits the rookies, what we're about to do. At this distance the kids look so normal, some instinct deep down still pushing the older ones to dress themselves, if only in rags.

GPS tells me we've slowed down some, and we're only a couple of miles from the castle. We're lucky here in Britain, if you can call it lucky. A lot of countryside, a lot of tall, old ruins, still easily scalable. What we do isn't as viable in the US – there are plenty of tall buildings, but they're too densely packed to allow visibility, and too hard for a kid to negotiate. And the children need to see the envelope from a way off or the exercise is a waste of time.

Course, they also have more guns over in the US, so maybe it isn't too much worse for them. But I don't know if I'd have the stomach for what needs doing, up that close.

Apparently, possession has been happening throughout human history, but most of the time it doesn't quite take; the possessing personalities aren't that strong or sophisticated. Adults are pretty sterile ground for whatever it is that's tried to take us over, and up until about fifteen years ago that meant that there were so few cases of full-term acquisition that most people didn't even know it happened, or believe that it did if they didn't see it for themselves.

Nobody knows exactly what changed, but it seems that the invaders – whoever they are – started thinking tactically. Instead of wasting their time and resources on abortive broad-spectrum attempts to take over *everyone*, they started focusing on the kids. Only the small ones – something happens to us at puberty that blocks them out – but pretty much every child from birth to around the age of eleven or twelve is lost to them.

The kids are stronger than they should be. A healthy adult can still, if he's vicious enough, physically overpower one of them, but most people don't have it in them to be that hard. And they're crafty – pretty much running on animal instinct, but capable of extreme acts of treachery. What's inside them doesn't have any sort of higher intelligence as we recognise it. At least none that's shown itself to us. But in most circumstances, one of them can do a lot more damage to one of us than we could have imagined ten years ago. And they seem to be able to sniff us out.

Some people are convinced that these kids have *powers*. That they can read minds, or spit fire and acid. Control you with a look. As if the malevolent cunning and strength aren't enough.

I spot Middleton Castle, in the distance but getting closer. I tap the rookie on the shoulder. She's transfixed by the children following us. I point out the castle, and she nods.

"There are hundreds of them. I lost count at two-fifty. How did there get to be so many?" she asks. I shrug. It's a question for another time. She's young, and cage-raised, and hasn't ever seen more than a half-dozen kids in any one place.

The adults had to run from the cities and towns and villages. In less than six months all of the children, the ones that physically could, had turned on the grown-ups. They beat us up, they tore at us. There are reports, though scattered, that they feed on us.

They never mastered vehicles, though, so we ran. And now we hide in safe havens, and our numbers drop, and we only breed in terror. Our babies are born under armed guard. Our children are kept in secure isolation until they are old enough to shake off the intruder, and their parents aren't allowed to go near the pens. Of course, we have to be careful, and… we lose some of them. Puberty is difficult to predict, and sometimes the other children realise that they're no longer possessed before we do. Turn on them.

We have no idea how this process works in the wild, or how their numbers seem to be increasing. Our scientists and our religious leaders and our politicians have their theories, but scouting missions don't ever return with anything useful, and the rest of us try not to think about it.

We're not even sure what value missions like the one the rookie and I are on right now have. We're just fulfilling a need to do *something*. Something terrible, yes. Something vile. But the only proactive thing we *can* do are these culls. Whether they have any long-term effect on the possessed population or not.

The envelope has to be yellow. Yellow or some other bright colour. See, something in them – either in the kids, or in the monsters inside them – is drawn to the brightness and contrast. And a hot-air balloon can move slowly enough that enough of the kids can keep up.

And then when we reach some high point, like a cliff or like this old stone tower that we've just arrived at, a balloon can maintain a relatively static position.

"They're… coming up the tower," says the rookie.

We like Middleton Castle, because it has these towers, and it still has usable stairs. The poor little bastards can climb pretty well, but it takes a lot longer that way. And the last thing you want to do on these missions is hang around. It plays too heavy on your soul.

The rookie watches in silence as the children make their way up the castle. As we hang there in the air more and more of them arrive, clustering in a swarm around the base of the building. It's a cloudless day and visibility is high so we seem to have picked up a good harvest. They crowd out in a broad arc in the direction we came from, only starting to thin out to stragglers a mile or so from us. In the other direction, odd locals who've spotted us since our arrival start to appear, coming toward the big yellow ball in the sky. Like kids *used* to flock toward balloons and the sound of the ice-cream van.

We both know what's coming – the rookie's briefing will have been thorough – but that doesn't stop each of us holding our breath as the first child makes it to the highest parapet, and falters there. Pulls themselves up onto the lip. We're out of reach, but are close enough that we can see her very clearly. A blonde girl in rags, only four or five. Her hair is thin, and wisps of it move in the breeze. And then she looks up at us, hands out, and we see her eyes. Dark, red, and angry. Thwarted and horrible.

She steps forward toward us, and is gone. Over the edge, down to hard stone below and rolling, rag-doll, away down the slope at the bottom of the wall. I'm not sure when I started breathing again, but I hear the rookie gasp out her first when the body hits the ground, far enough away that we don't hear it.

They are stronger than children, and us, and they may have powers, but their hosts are still fragile, and as far as we can tell mortal.

And then more children are at the ledge, and we can hear their screams of frustration, and anguish gives way to fear. It doesn't matter how safe we are here; the basket still feels too low. More children start to go over until it's hard to even see them as anything more than a heaving mass any more. The bodies gather in drifts at the bottom of the slope, high enough that the possessed coming from that direction struggle to climb over them.

But eventually they do. Eventually all of the ones that we can see make it to the top, and go over the edge.

We haven't spoken since that first blonde girl. It's more than two hours from then to the last straggler going over. We stay in place for the whole time, following our orders to watch every one fall, and the official reason for that is due diligence but everyone who ever completes one of these missions knows that it's really a sort of memorial.

These are still our children, after all.

When the last has fallen, we head for open water and higher altitude, the only secure way to return to safe haven. The rookie has done well to maintain her composure, and I tell her so.

You Go To Bed, You Wake Up

It's the dream you have where you go to bed and you wake up.

You wake up, you get up, you get showered and dressed and on the bus. You go to work.

You get middle-managed. You brushed your teeth. You should have mentioned you brushed your teeth. You forget breakfast.

You wake up.

You go to bed, you wake up.

You had your whole day, and you worked and you slacked off and you got line-managed and you got annoyed and you had a laugh but there were more annoyances than there were laughs and on balance it was a balanced day but it cost you more than it made you and you went to bed ready for five or six or seven or eight hours sleep and you woke up.

You said too much but you didn't say enough and you took too much of it to feel like a person but you didn't smile enough while you did it so you're still a problem to the people that you shouldn't be a problem to but you still feel compromised. You went to work and you went to bed and you woke up.

In the dream you don't remember kissing your lover that day. There are no kids in the dream; no love at all. But it's still a day long, and it is as exhausting as a day with love in it. You come home from work, you sit on the sofa til too late and drag yourself to bed dog-tired. You wake up.

You brush your teeth and get dressed and on the bus. You don't remember waiting for the bus in the dream and you're at work. You get micro-managed. You don't know it's a dream, so you sit there. You can't hear a word anybody is saying, but everybody is talking at you. Their mouths are moving and you're filling time with placeholder words trying to work out what you're supposed to say. It's like being awake but you spend the day and the day spends you and you go home and decide on an early night but stay up too late and you go to bed and you wake up.

You think you're cool with yourself; you like yourself; you're down. But you can't be, because your dreams won't let you answer back or walk out or blow up or sashay your ass out flipping fingers left and right. You sit and seethe and it costs you and you go to bed to recharge and your head hits the pillow and you close your eyes and it's morning.

Balance

I carry this thing in my pocket which makes everything worthwhile.

The place where I work is a vast edifice on the edge of the financial district. It is one of seven similar buildings owned by the company that I work for. The company that I work for has three names, and they are the names of the men who formed the company. If anyone with one of those names still remains, it is probably only as shareholders now.

There are six hundred and thirty-two people working for the company in this building, though there are a further sixty-eight employed by agencies that the company employs, to feed us and clean up after us.

I am a quantity surveyor for the company. I survey quantities. I count things. I have been working here for more than eight years. I loathe my job, though not enough to leave it. There is a delicate balance in this equation, and I am not at the tipping point. At least half of the people in my office are over that point, but stay anyway.

My office, as a collective, hates all of the other offices, collectively, though each person in it has friends in those other offices. Each person is at least three people: The person who is a percentage of their office, the person who fiercely guards their own desk-space from their office mates, and the person who they are at home. Sometimes the three people are very different from each other, other times the same but for a few insignificant details.

Of the six hundred and thirty-two people who work here for the company, one hundred and two earn between them slightly more than the other five hundred and thirty combined. And only fifteen act with real authority, though many more are paid to manage.

'Manage' is a funny word. It suggests control and authority, but broken down and examined, it can mean the same thing as 'cope'.

There is a person, somewhere in the building, whose job it is to buy art to line the corridors and decorate the meeting rooms. They are very good at their job, and despite the corporate sterility of the company and its buildings, beautiful things hang on the eggshell walls, taunting us.

In the foyer one particular piece enthrals me. It is a large, square canvas, with brass brushwork over black across its surface. Laid out in perfect rows and columns, in relief, are tiny little plaster men, painted dirty gold, rough and in a variety of poses. Some of them are upright, some point down, and though they are equally spaced but jumbled in order, the ones looking up are equal in number to the ones that are falling. There are exactly a hundred tiny people.

The company itself is no worse than any other company, and the jobs within are no worse than any other jobs, but for most of the people working here, being no worse is not enough to spark enthusiasm. It is the tragedy of the middle class that they are as pinned to the centre of their lives by their finances as the very poor or the very rich, rewarded well enough that deserting isn't an option, but not well enough to buy themselves a little control.

But nobody weeps for the middle classes, and they shouldn't.

Lack of control is a big part of corporate life, here, and down here at the midway point of the workforce, sometimes the only way to gain control is to take it.

The painting is a grid. There is a mathematical formula for the way the eye drifts across it, or the brain processes the small people on it, or the point at which a person stops seeing each one on its own, and just sees a crowd, but it would be hard to write it down, and it would be slightly different for each person looking. People aren't all the same height, and don't all have the same attention span.

My job is also a calling, and I have a natural knack for these things. I instinctively know that there is a point, toward the bottom and the right, where, if one of the men were plucked from the canvas, breaking the tiny plaster bond holding it there, nobody would notice that it was gone.

So now I walk through my working days with one of the tiny people hidden in my pocket. I picked it out based on overall placement, and have since forgotten whether it was rising up or falling down, but it is enough to know that I have disrupted the balance. I don't dwell long enough in front of the painting to count them out any more, and free of the wall the little guy is neutral, held in my hand, in my pocket, in free-fall.

Dougie Lets Himself Go

So, I'm in this greasy spoon, down on Mary Street. It was back when I was doing temp work, and as last-lad-on-the-job I was out shopping for everyone's mid-morning fried-egg and mushroom sandwiches.

I wasn't foreign to the area so I knew well enough to keep myself to myself, sat at one of the tables nearest the counter, waiting for the sarnies to be made. Head down, half-listening to the banter of the old woman and tall, tanned and handsome guy behind the counter. At odds utterly with the clientele and area, the two of them sounded like preening old biddies working in a local hairdresser.

This was back when those places were still as permeated with cigarette smoke as bacon fat. I've never been a smoker, but I've always been certain that certain food just tastes better when it's made in grimy places. The sheer volume of fried-egg, cheese and mushroom sandwiches I ate back then only bolster that viewpoint.

After a while the guy waved me over and I went up to receive the grease-spotted paper bags full of oily bounty.

As I went to leave someone near the door called my name.

It was Dougie.

He was sitting at a table with his back to the big window that fronted the place, which was why I hadn't noticed him before. I hadn't seen him in a while, and he didn't look good.

"Alright, mate?" he called, ever genial. He pushed the seat opposite him out with his foot, inviting me to sit. It'd been a while since I'd seen him, so I sat.

We talked for a bit, catching up. But we could both tell that I was distracted by the stuff on the table in front of him.

On his plate – and bear in mind this was around ten in the morning – was a half-eaten double cheeseburger, slippery mushroom and onion making themselves known under the saturated bap. The unreal yellow of the cheese punctuated brightly by the acid redness of ketchup squirted from the tomato-shaped plastic dispenser on the table. The burger dominated the plate, but the rest of it was crammed full of chips, fried egg, and beans.

Which was striking on its own. Combined with the half-smoked cigarette in the little foil ashtray that he kept taking drags from, the can of lager next to his coffee mug, and the carrier bag full of its siblings on one of the other chairs, it made a slightly shocking tableau.

"Blimey, Dougie, you look well," I said, and the grin on my face told him different.

The thing is I've known plenty of walking car-crashes, but Dougie hadn't ever been one of them. He liked a drink, and a smoke, but he was always in pretty good shape compared to the rest of us.

But now he looked like shit. His cheeks were puffy from over-eating, but drawn and dry from chain smoking. When he shifted in his seat you could tell that his previously imposing frame was all off-kilter; round at the belly, thinned out at the wrists.

He grinned and said, "Yeah, looking good, eh?" then took a massive, painful looking bite out of the burger.

"Steady on, mate!" I said. I knew it wasn't really any of my business, but fear that he might choke himself made me blurt it out.

"Ah, it's alright," he said, after forcing the food down, "I'll get hit by a bus tomorrow."

"I suppose," I said, but I was worried. I watched him take another puff. Then I remembered the bag of sandwiches, and started feeling the pull of obligation. I stood up, and said, "I'd better go, mate. Good seeing you, though, yeah?"

He nodded, a big smile on his face. "You too, mate."

I'd got all the way to the door before I twigged what he'd actually said.

"You mean, 'I *might* get hit by a bus tomorrow,'" I said to the back of his head. He shrugged.

"Yeah, maybe," he said. Chuckled darkly. "Or maybe I know something you don't."

I laughed, though afterwards I wasn't entirely sure why. It had seemed to be the right thing to do.

I never saw Dougie again.

The Short Cut Through

Carlisle sat on the bench waiting. Autumn drizzled against his jacket as he listened to the splashing water of the memorial fountain. The sound lulled him.

"You know, that thing wasn't working all summer."

The voice broke across his meditative wanderings, and he looked around to find the source. It was the man he was here to meet.

"Various reasons. Health and safety fears that someone would slip on the cobbles. That there was a water shortage. Other stuff."

"Shame." Carlisle responded, getting to his feet. "Still, summer's loss, eh?"

They stood together in silence for a few moments watching the arcs of water gushing up from the ground, splashing down into the circle's gutter, a testament to a woman that most people remembered best watching her cry on television. The ripples from the fountain-fall were intense and loud, but those of the worsening drizzle had the strength of numbers.

"You're James?" said Carlisle.

"Afraid so." The man replied, giving a sad nod as he spoke.

"Shall we walk? I know you wanted to meet here, but there isn't much for shelter. Besides," he nodded away from the fountain, "I'd like to visit the site."

James agreed, so they began to walk.

It wasn't long before they got where they were going. They took shelter in a sad-looking bandstand near their destination. Neither could remember ever seeing anyone play here, despite its prominent spot in the town. They looked across a short distance to a fenced-off demolition site, at rest in the early evening. The massive yellow machines in there were washed grey and skeletal in the dimness.

Muddy light came down from a plastic-covered bulb in the dome of the bandstand. James watched as Carlisle took a folded piece of paper out of his pocket and opened it out, revealing a photocopied photograph. The image had the tell-tale dots of something printed in a newspaper and then blown-up. He held it up, offering a side-by-side comparison with the diggers and cranes, and the rubble.

"Looks different, doesn't it?" James said, and Carlisle nodded.

James didn't seem to want to look at the photo, but Carlisle took it in again for what seemed like the hundredth time since finding it earlier that day in the library archives. It showed a squared-off tunnel, dark, the detail you *could* see revealing it as one of those throwbacks to the architectural misery of the sixties – a passageway through a brutal concrete building, the sides made of dirty glass, most of it boarded over, which told you that these had been shops but were now deserted shells.

Carlisle remembered it well – everyone in Southerton over a certain age did – as the Lewis building. It had been the largest department store most people in town had ever seen, situated a stone's throw from the city centre proper. And then it had been empty for nearly a decade, when the distance it took to throw a stone seemed too far to go for quality goods and sundries, and nobody thought much about it except as a huge, dirty obstacle between the park and the pubs.

The tunnel in the photo had been the only shortcut through it. Going through there had always been a slightly surreal experience – you entered from greenery into darkness, and exited onto a brightly lit and wide-open space, the sun reflecting off the bright marbled frontage of the council buildings nearby. In the photo the other side was an intense, bright square, with a cluster of three or four people silhouetted at the exit. Or the entrance, Carlisle had thought.

"You took the photo, then, huh?"

"Yeah." James replied. "The people in it, they were my friends. Harris told you that, right?"

Carlisle nodded, and said "I'm sorry."

"No, it's okay. Does it sound callous if I tell you that I barely remember them, now?"

"No, I understand. Without Facebook I wouldn't remember the people I know from week to week, let alone nearly ten years."

James had grinned at that. Carlisle smiled, then grimaced. He hated asking the hard questions. "Can I ask what you remember about the day itself? When you took the photo?" Carlisle took the pause as an opportunity to re-fold the piece of paper and slide it back into his pocket.

"I guessed that that was why you wanted to meet me, Mr Carlisle. Honestly though, as I told the police back then there isn't really much to tell. We were on our way to the pub for lunch – we'd had a full morning of lectures, so a pint was practically compulsory – and we were going through the cut-through.

I had hung back to check my phone – a text message had come through, and the Lewis building was always a bugger for reception. I read it, looked up, and saw that the others had walked on a way ahead of me. And… this sounds daft, I know, but you remember when phones first started having cameras on them? And when you got your first one, suddenly you were taking pictures of bloody everything. Even if you already had a proper camera?" Carlisle nodded.

"So, anyway, there they were, and it was noon, so the sun must have been on the other side of the building, and the light was just incredible. So, I thought, I'm having that. My phone was already out, so I popped the camera bit open, and took the picture. I didn't take my time over it, either.

If I'd known it was going to be in the papers…"

James paused for a moment. Carlisle was starting to wonder whether he should prompt him when he started talking again.

"…And so, I ran – half jogged, honestly – to catch up to them. And they weren't there. Or anywhere on the street that I could see. I mean, I hadn't been that far behind, and there wasn't anywhere that they could have gone without running for it.

Course, that's what I'd thought they'd done, as a joke or something. I went on to the pub, cursing them, and didn't think anything of it. When they didn't show up there, or for their afternoon lectures, I started feeling a little left out – I guess I thought they'd skived off back home or somewhere. I didn't start to think anything was properly up until the next day when they hadn't surfaced. Then the day after that, the police showed up, asking questions.

It turned out I was the last person to see them. And I haven't thought about it much in years, but I guess if you're here, they never did actually turn up, eh?"

Carlisle nodded.

"Lisa Brevin's parents hired me. I don't think they expect much, but, you know…" He waved a hand at the demolition works. "I guess they heard about this, and felt like they had to give it one last try. You shouldn't feel bad about it… I think they're just looking for one last reason to give up."

"S'probably just something totally mundane and horrible that happened to them, you know? Millions of reasons and ways to vanish, aren't there?" James said, a shrug in his voice. "It's stupid to think that the tunnel had anything to do with it. It's not like the Pied Piper came down and spirited them away through some magic portal to Narnia."

Carlisle looked at him, eyebrow raised. James noticed this, and laughed hard.

"Sorry. Stupid, I know, but at the time I was doing my dissertation on repeating story tropes in kids' books. That story was on my mind. I used to sometimes think of myself as... the kid that got left behind. There's almost always one."

"Oh." Carlisle said. Not much else to say.

"Still, funny to think isn't it? A tunnel, or a gateway, it's just an absence of stuff. An open door is just an unfilled hole. It's strange to think that now that they're finally pulling the Lewis building down, the cut-through is gone. When it wasn't ever really there in the first place. When that was the whole point of it."

As he spoke, James was looking intently at a single point somewhere beyond the fence, where Carlisle guessed the tunnel must have been.

Carlisle had already decided that he was going to offer to buy the man a pint for his trouble. Now, he was uncomfortably aware of the two of them here in the deserted park, so near to the half-gone building. As the evening darkened the need for warmth, alcohol and the sound of raised voices suddenly seemed much more important.

If We Leave Right Now, It'll Always Be A Party

I'm on my way from one job to another, on foot because it's nearby and rushing because I'm late, when I glance into a music-shop window and all urgency saps out of my stride. There's something there in the centre of the display that I recognise. That reminds me of Eve.

-

She was still beautiful the last time I saw her, though you could see where it was straining – the points on her skin where the bad things inside her would most likely break through first. She looked like she looked good for her age, if she was ten years older than she was.

The last time we really spoke properly she'd still had the charm, but her eyes moved that little bit too fast, and her speech that bit too slow. Like she was out of sync with herself.

That was at my place, the house on Avenue Avenue where I lived alone. Before Jim and I moved in together, into the bigger place with room for a nursery. She had invited herself round but I was glad to see her, and we shared a bottle of wine and some memories, though she was drinking faster than I.

Midway through her second glass I had asked her how she was feeling, but I'd obviously done a bad job of masking the *real* question because she had shaken her head slowly, her hand up to me, a denial of an accusation that I thought I'd managed not to make.

She didn't answer either question, though.

"Did you ever see that film, 'Leaving Las Vegas'?" She had asked instead.

-

We had watched it together, one night a few years before.

Back then we had been inseparable. At the time I could match her drink for drink, drug for drug, come-down for come-down.

If she was the wild one, it was just another of the chaotic things in our chaotic world that she had complete control of. So, it seemed to me. She always had money to burn on the things we loved, and she always had a plan. I followed in her wake, her holding tight onto my hand so that I wouldn't get swept away. It seemed to me.

It wasn't until later that I realised that she had the money to burn because she couldn't ever hold on to any, or anything. And she could make the plans because she never thought beyond the end of the night.

And besides, those plans – though she seemed so wise to me at the time – never broke particularly new ground. They generally either involved watching DVDs with a bottle of vodka on her ratty sofa in her shitty flat, or going out to one of a small selection of pubs and clubs, flirting with boys or kissing each other on the dance-floor for drinks and giggles.

Sometimes she'd change it up a little. She'd pull out her guitar, bright pink and covered with stickers – omnipresent in the corner of the room, always on display, seldom used – and she'd play me songs, mostly covers but very occasionally stuff she'd written herself. Broken, angry, sad songs that she'd laugh off afterwards.

She'd bought the guitar when she was younger, saved up for it out of the pocket money she'd earned during a childhood she never talked about. As she told it, it was money she was saving to escape from something. But she had bought the guitar instead.

She would sing low, and only for me. Honestly, though, I think she was only really singing for herself.

It was a crazy time, and it had taken a lot of time for me to grow past it. Still, I don't know if I've ever found life as easy or as fun as I felt it was during that time, and if that was because we were too drunk or high on each other to know any different… Well, I don't know if that really diminishes the feeling.

So, one night we were lying on the sofa, slumped across each other as often happened, passing a bottle back and forth and watching the film. It's about a guy who decides to drink himself to death, and decides to do it in Vegas. On the way he meets a prostitute and takes her along, but really she's not part of his story – she's just there to have someone there in the film to feel bad about his situation, as he doesn't give much of a fuck about it himself and he's driven everyone else he knew *before* we meet him away.

We watched, and drank. As the story played out, I absent-mindedly stroked the band of Kanji symbols on Eve's exposed tummy up to the point where the tattoo sunk below her belt.

Back then we were fierce and brave, and our love flickered and burst like a fire – sometimes we were friends, and sometimes something else.

She was my one big gay crush. My bi try. Looking back, I'm really not sure what I was to her. She called me 'Angel' because she knew I hated

'Ange' even more than I hated 'Angela', and at the time that felt enough like a sign of love for me.

The film made me cry. It made Eve cry too, and we talked about it for hours afterwards until we both passed out on the sofa.

At the time we felt so aligned, but whenever I remembered that night, I wondered whether we'd really watched the same movie.

-

"We watched it together." I had responded, trying not to sound too hurt that she didn't remember. "Hm." She pantomimed thinking about it as she sipped some more wine. "Did we?"

She put the glass down, and returned to her point.

"Here's the thing about 'Leaving Las Vegas'. It's a pretty bleak film, right?"

"I wasn't sure you'd noticed, but yes. Very sad indeed."

"Yes, but… but… here's the thing. If you watch the film through, but just… *stop paying attention* – switch it off or leave the room or whatever – before the final act, it's *actually* a film about a guy going on a trip and having a good time."

I looked at her, a little stunned at her expectant smile.

"No. No, Eve, it really isn't." I said. The smile left her face and her eyes darted to one side before coming back to stare at me, a little colder than I was used to seeing them. Her chin jutted like a child's.

"Well, I think it is." She said. "If you don't like how something's going, you should just leave the room before it ends, Angela."

She left me alone with the empty bottle soon afterwards. I only saw her a few times after that, in pubs and just around, but never to speak to. I knew that she was still in town because people would mention bumping into her, but she never got in touch. And then after a while I didn't hear anything anymore.

-

Standing staring in the window at the bright pink guitar, I can tell that I'm crying. Nothing too showy or embarrassing, no sobbing. Just a few silent tears, wet cheeks.

I look at my watch, see that I've been here a couple of minutes but I'm not yet late. The thing about present-day me, I'm always ahead of time. I've always left a margin for error.

There's no doubt that it's Eve's guitar in the window. It's been cleaned up some, but there's an image of a cartoon cat right there, under the strings. I'd only ever seen it sneaking out between band logos and pop-culture slogans, but it's uniquely *her*; a friend had painted it on for her while she was at college.

I walk this way a lot, and I hadn't seen it before today. I'm not sure what this means. If it's here, now, Eve must still be around too. But if it's here, now, this thing that she gave up her future for, what does that mean? Didn't she need it any more, or could she just not afford to hang on to it?

I put my hand to the glass, picturing her moments after selling the guitar, standing right where I am. I almost see her reflection sliding over mine, looking down on her most beloved possession behind the glass.

I realise that I'm thinking about going inside and buying Eve's guitar, though I've never even played.

A Mate Like Barry

"Sorry motherfucker," Barry says by way of greeting.

He sits down opposite me, putting his pint down in front of him, and does the middle-aged grunt as he settles in place.

"You didn't get me one, then?" I say.

"Well, it seemed rude to assume, as it was on your tab."

"Perfect," I reply, and stare back down into my almost dead drink.

It's hard to stay depressed with Barry around, but I manage it fine for a while. He has this way of acting like he hasn't noticed or doesn't care that your life is shit. He acts that way because he doesn't care or notice that your life is shit.

"Things are bad, but they aren't worse, mate'" he says, after getting a few more rounds in on my tab. It's not something I want to hear from him. "You need to snap out of it." He rubs his left thumb and index finger together, back and forth. "Only the tiniest violin in the world plays for the dumped boyfriend."

"I've seen that film," I reply, dismissive. "And I wasn't her boyfriend, I was her husband." I glare at him. "And I wasn't *dumped*. She fucked somebody else for the whole time we were together, and then chucked me out of my *own house* when she got bored of lying about it."

He slumps back in his chair, and shrugs.

"Well, yeah. But I mean, it's not like you have cancer," he says. And then plays the world's smallest violin for me again, hand held over his drink.

"Jesus," I say, rolling my eyes. His indifference to my pain has the odd effect of making it seem like too much work to feel the pain in the first place. I watch him for a moment as he rubs his fingers together absent-mindedly.

"You need to better manage your expectations. Adjust your perspective," Barry says. "Like, to a little kid, the world's smallest violin is just the right size. And to a midget, it's like a cello."

"A little person."

"Yeah, a little person."

"No, I mean, I don't think you're supposed to call them 'midgets.'"

"Whatever." A muffled chirp has him squirming in his seat, trying to get at his jeans pocket. "Or a baby!" he blurts, distracted.

"What are you on about?"

"To a baby. To a baby, the world's smallest violin looks like a cello, or a double bass."

We sit in silence for a minute as he fishes out his phone and checks his texts.

"Ah, bollocks. I need to go mate. You know how it is with girlfriends." He starts getting up, collecting himself.

"Wives. How it is with wives," I correct him.

"Hah! That's a perspective thing, though, innit?" he says, laughing, and it makes me want to punch him, but at the same time it makes my anger and dismay seem like a waste of everyone's time.

"Anyway, better get back before she loses her rag. You know what she's like."

"Why would a baby have anything to do with a fucking violin?" I blurt to his swiftly diminishing back, and then into my pint I mutter a goodbye.

And I stay in the pub and drink some more, but the mixture of scattered laughter and emotional neglect that Barry visited on me stays, and I'm no longer sad, or angry. At the very most I'm numb, and bored of ennui.

I have to wonder, because there's nothing else to do when you're left to your own company, if everyone doesn't have a mate like Barry. The sort of mate who it doesn't matter how shit you feel, they always leave you feeling less bad, if not actually better. The sort of mate who can sleep in your bed, and steal your wife, and never get a round in with his own money, and feel so little shame about it that your own self-righteous anger seems absurd, and all you're left with is a huge bar tab and a big empty.

Last Orders

"If you aren't fucking her that just makes it weirder, though…" someone says, a bit loud, and everyone who hears either knows what he's talking about or makes a mental note to find out later.

But it soon sinks back into the noise of the night, drink and chatter clouding memories, smoke filling the corners of the dark little basement bar, soaking up detail and the sharp edges of everyone's voices and faces.

The usual bunch are mostly present, even though it's a school night. The girls from finance are in one of the booths, you recognise a few people standing at the bar from other nights and other bars.

The lady from Sainsbury's who laughs and sings and chatters to herself while she collects the baskets is dressed up nice and crying quietly in a corner, the bar staff drawing straws on who'll next serve her.

The group you're approximately here with are taking up the tables in the middle. From where you're sitting, drinking and drinking it all in, you can see everyone.

Lucy is back in town for the week, she and Pete at a table nearby, trying to catch up while not talking about anything important. Everyone else is arranged around one long table, like the last supper if Jesus had said "this is weird, we can't look at each other properly, some of you go round the other side".

If Jesus was a big twat called Simon who never says anything intelligent, but wants everyone to hear him say it.

So, Simon, then Ruby, David, Rosie, Abraham, Julian (and his wife Julianne), Fat David (who lost weight and is now thinner than the other David), Jonty, and two girls Simon got talking to at the bar who let him drag them over. And Pete and Lucy at the next table.

And you.

Simon has dropped his cock piercing into the conversation.

Nobody was talking about sex, or him, or piercings… you think one of the girls might have been talking about wedding venues? But Simon persists, because that is what Simon does. When neither of the girls responds to mention of his piercing, he acts like they did anyway, and keeps talking about it.

He even adds a little eye-roll, as if strange girls in pubs are always banging on about his piercing. It is transparent as fuck to anyone who cares to see it, but everyone lets it slide because the frenetic nature of the night allows that luxury.

People are better in hazy rooms; most of us aren't meant to be seen too clearly. But you notice a ripple of dismay move through everyone who knows him. Julianne's face wrinkles in disgust, and Fat David and David both drop their heads at the exact same moment and stop making eye contact with anyone else for a few minutes, like twins.

You hear Lucy mutter "Cunt" under her breath, and that shocks Pete, who didn't think she and Simon even knew each other that well.

"Come on…" he says, the cogs turning, because he doesn't remember her like this and he's trying to work out if this is how she was when she left, or if living away has changed her, "…it's just Simon, you know?"

Over at the big table the girls are trying to change the subject, because there is nothing worse than unsolicited cock and that's even when it's just in conversation, but their social programming takes hold and they laugh despite themselves at Simon's jokes and he takes that as consent.

And now he's standing up, his hands on his belt, but he's tutting at the same time, saying "fucksake, go on then!" as if it's under protest. Because one thing you know is that there are two kinds of men with cock piercings: the ones you will probably never, ever know about, and the ones who want to show you but want you to think it's a giant hassle.

He's making a show of it, sweeping arm movements, as his zip opens and he pulls his jeans down for clearance. Despite yourself you glance over, the drama suggesting greatness, making you curious.

Finally, he stands revealed, hands on his hips, depressed genitals not quite dwarfed by showy jewellery, but he's only on display for a second, and people gasping, because suddenly the view is blocked.

While everyone else was looking in every other direction, Lucy has snagged up Pete's pint glass, half full or half empty with piss-weak lager depending on how you look at it, and crossed the distance to Simon.

She punches at him with it, somewhere soft enough that you expect the rim of the curve of the glass to sink inside without breaking, but it breaks and everything breaks, always, and she's punching at him there with it again, but now the edge of the glass is jagged and broken like the look in her eyes and it bites into his flesh, inside inside inside and she keeps at him. He's screaming and she's screaming and everybody else in the place is screaming and the whole world is screaming too.

Works

The scaffolding started going up at around half-seven this morning.

There's always construction work going on in the city, so no-one really noticed the noise over the traffic until the structure started going up in front of our windows. The sound of boots and metal on metal pressed in over the persistent hum of computers and air-conditioners.

That happened at around 10 here on the third floor, although it's difficult to give an exact time with any certainty: this side of the building is away from the street and only has very small, high-up windows, so it could have been going up from a little earlier round the front and we wouldn't have seen it.

Anyway, around then-ish, one of us asked our office manager what was going on, just out of interest. He shrugged, suggested it was just a bit of cosmetic surgery for the distressed concrete 1950s carbuncle, and strode off to do something managerial and important in a different part of the office.

That seemed reasonable enough. The stretch-and-compression of 50 odd years of nights and days had etched long, thin hairline cracks into the grey finish; nothing too worrying structurally, but if you looked close at the front of the building you could easily see them.

Curiosity sated, we went back to work.

Out on the street buying lunch at noon, I looked around to see if I could find any of the scaffolders or workmen that had turned the day into such a mess of clanking, cluttering and criss-crossing shadows. By now the structure reached so high that it almost took on an identity of its own, separate from our building. Up around the eighth floor it continued to grow but the noon sun, so high in the sky, threw the workers totally into shadow so that they were little more than a mess of movement and furtive noise up there.

It was easy to imagine the cold, dark and fibrous structure growing organically in the heat and humidity of the day.

I shook that particular nasty thought off, threw my crusts down for the birds, and went back to work.

At around 3.30 a rumour started to flutter down from the IT guys that the work was continuing on past the 18th floor. One of them was up working in management (that's the top floor, 20) and had been able to look down on the approaching upper platforms of the structure from the windows there.

Word came down with them that it was a bigger job than we'd first thought; that there might be structural work being done. As is typical hereabouts, actual solid information was difficult to come by about a functional thing like that. If someone from accounts had had sex with someone from marketing, news of it would spill down the corridors like floodwater, instantly reaching every point in the building. But anything it would be useful to know moves slow.

By 4.30 we no longer noticed the long, geometric, alien shadows that the bars threw across each office. The noise had subsided as construction continued upwards until there was only the smallest irregular vibration singing down to us along the tubes from high above. Now even that had stopped and the only noise was the lazy tapping of fingers on keyboards and the last minute clicking of mouse-buttons in the afternoon heat.

And then at 5, the daily exodus. But today, those of us that put in till exactly 5-o-clock spilled into the building's reception area only to find the slackers who habitually left ten minutes early standing, vexed and irritable, in front of tightly closed doors. Bewildered muttering escalated to agitated flustering as each new arrival compulsively checked and rechecked the firmness of each door, despite the obvious dark weight of the scaffolding showing through the textured glass.

Caretakers were called, keys were tried, and by about 6 panic started to bubble through the ranks. The odd managers who remained at work on the upper floors were called, but they didn't have a clue what might be going on, and some even threatened dire consequences if the situation hadn't been sorted when they were ready to leave for home.

By 7:30 they were all sitting in the foyer with the rest of us.

People had started crying earlier when we realised that all outside phone-lines were down. Their will might have been stronger had it not been for a workday spent under the oppressive weight of all that metal.

Despite the best efforts of the IT guys the internet was no longer accessible, and the scaffolding seemed to be interfering with mobile signals, too. By the time someone had thought to try to get out onto the roof, no-one was particularly surprised to find that all roof access points were blocked.

Everyone stopped expecting to be rescued around an hour ago. I don't know if it's something to do with the structure, or something that we've worked up to subconsciously over the days and months and years of our relentless rhythmic existence in this place. But each in our own way we seemed to quietly realise that this building and everything in it needs some work done. Is mostly obsolete. Needs a top-to-bottom renovation.

At some point someone has raided the kitchens scattered around departments, and someone else has started passing mugs of tea to anyone who wants them. Biscuits have been found, by God! Distracted, I have lost at least two halves to the depths of my mug, but at least I know that they're waiting for me when I reach the bottom.

I just hope I have time.

Twenty minutes ago, exactly midnight, work restarted. The sound reaches us as distant grinding and screeching, but it's getting louder all the time. The sounds of deconstruction. The sounds of reconstruction.

I wonder what will be put here in our place?

The Same Three Tunes

She sits at the baby grand piano in the corner
of the room, catching the sun, and in sharp
contrast against it.

She plays three tunes.
She plays the same three tunes.
She only plays the same three tunes.

An old jazz solo that she loved enough to
search out the sheet music for.
A Michael Nyman piece that you were so proud
of yourself for recognising, until you realised
that you knew it from an advert.
The bit of Danse Macabre that you hadn't
heard before.

She only ever plays the same three tunes.
She only ever plays those same three tunes,
because those are the only three tunes that she
ever learned.

Before she was gone.

...But Then She Came Back

David sat on the floor, preoccupied with the beam of light cutting through the room, remembering childhood visits to the cinema. Back then each screen was like a proper theatre and people smoked everywhere. David would find himself distracted looking up there toward the high ceiling, seeing the film caught and reversed in a bright beam of light above him, the story playing out in smoke that you didn't even realise was there. Until years later, when it was gone.

His eyes prickled and he found himself sniffing involuntarily. He rubbed the back of his arm across his nose as he snorted, looking up at her.

"Oh, please, don't cry. *Don't*." Sally said. She paused. Then asked, not unkindly. "Why do you think that I left you?"

She looked away from him, looked out of the window onto the night with its huddled, clamouring, tiny clusters of people – the shouts and the squeals. A mist rolled through the streets, thick enough to catch the light, still thin enough that you could see the groups as they ran and jumped and laughed and cried.

"I don't know." David spluttered. "Because I'm weak?" More petulant than weak.

It looked like bonfire night come a few days early. In places in the distance the sky glowed orange. It was midnight, but the streets were moonlit white. You had to look up to see the darkness in the sky, the blank slate of the streets dissipating like steam up into it.

"No, darling. You're not listening. I'm asking you to think really hard about it, because I really want to know the truth. Why do you believe that I left you?" She looked back around at him, fixing him with sharp green eyes. "I need to know. I've been thinking about it a lot."

She looked back out into the bright and hazy night.

"Hey," she said, and he could see the bright smile on her face in the set of her jaw as she faced away from him, "do you remember New Years? The Minellium?"

He let the mistake go. It even brightened him a little. It was a fondly remembered foible. He nodded, and started to push himself up off the floor. She caught the movement on her periphery and half turned to grin at him.

"It looks just like it out there. Remember? All the smoke from the bonfires? The chaos and the joy?"

Somebody on one of the nearby streets started screaming – a high, persistent and sustained effort by somebody to shred their own throat. Sally's face creased in discomfort, a shudder of vestigial fear running through her as the sound echoed hollow off the semi-detached rows.

Standing and watching her close, now, David was struck by how beautiful she still was, even after all these years. Her long arms and slender wrists pale as ever, and he knew they'd be cold to the touch because they always were. Her face and neck a Modigliani, white in this light.

The spasm that ran through her sent a fine cloud of what looked like talc in a wave across her body, a momentary halo around her.

It didn't remind him of the end of the century.

Instead it made him think of that *other* end of the world a year later, when the planes hit the towers and the streets of New York became a world of white ash. The sight of the people walking out of the hell of it, a layer of it over them and over everything, in among all the horror of that day.

At the time he had said to Sally that it was weird how crisp and clean it made everything look; crystalline. Her love had distilled her response down into a raised eyebrow, before burying her face back into the desperate embrace they were in for that whole day.

He'd read later that the dust had killed a lot of people years after. Made a lot of others ill. By then, he had a new insight into loss, a new understanding of how the world worked.

The rarefied beauty that you found in the world would always kill you. Or else, it'd die. He had learnt that when his *own* world ended.

He looked at Sally, the dust finally settling again, her lovely smile complete, and he knew what she was really asking. A different "why?" from the one that he had been asking the universe since those long weeks in the hospital.

"Why did I think that you *left* me?" He said, his voice cracking as his fingers reached up to cup her cheek. "Because you went away, and I was still here." His other hand moved to her hip – slid around to ease her into a hug. She felt softer than he thought she would. He half expected her to fall apart under his touch – he had watched it happen once before.

"I would never leave you, silly man!" She smiled close into his ear. "And even if I did, you know that it doesn't count as long as I come home to you."

Sally's arms went around him, strong and sure, and if any of the smoke and ash of her fell away as they held each other it didn't matter. As the dust fell away, they breathed her back in.

"Pretty soon we'll all have come back," she whispered, dry lips on his skin. "…and then we'll *all* go away. Maybe somewhere better. And we'll go together."

A siren began its whine and echoed hollow, somewhere outside. Outside, the city screamed and ran and laughed and danced and cried – the chaos of a million and more wishes and dreams and nightmares come true.

Bindweed Creeps

When you come down to breakfast that morning your wife greets you with a scowl, careful not to let the boy see. He keeps pushing cornflakes around his bowl chattering to himself, although he seems more muted than usual. You lean over and kiss the top of his head, and flash her a bewildered look. You've no idea why she seems so annoyed. After all, you were on nightmare duty last night, and when your son started screaming you were up and out to his side before she'd even had a chance to stir that much.

"What's wrong?" you mouth at her.

She stands up calmly, and says "Daddy, can you help me get my coat on, please?"

"Good boys help put their coats on nicely!" the boy pipes up.

"Yes, that's right, they do," you say to him, moving out into the hallway to where your wife is already waiting. "Mummy and daddy will be back in five seconds."

"He had another nightmare last night," your wife tells you, voice low.

"Yes. I know," you say a little impatiently. "I was the one up at three in the morning comforting him."

"Oh, yeah?" she hisses slightly. "And did you ask him what he was dreaming about?"

"Of course I didn't!" you respond defensively. "We agreed that until he's a bit older it's better to distract him til he drops back off! He usually just forgets about it by morning."

"Well, fine. But this time he didn't. He's been crying on and off about it since he woke up."

"Shit. What did he dream about?"

You know before she tells you. He was dreaming about bindweed. He dreamed about wiry plants climbing up from under the grass, first sneaking around his feet, then up his legs… across his tiny chest, and finally choking him, dragging him down.

He wasn't able to describe it in nearly that much detail, but you know that's how the dream went. You've been having the same one for years.

"So, where the hell did he get all that from?" she barely manages to whisper.

"I don't know," you say sincerely, but are surprised to find errant guilt still pricking your cheeks.

"You *don't know*?" she snaps back in disbelief.

"I *don't!* Why would I have ever talked to a four-year-old about my bloody dreams?" you argue.

"Mummy, have you got your coat on yet?" the high voice asks from the kitchen.

You really don't know why your son is having the same dreams that haunt you. You've always been so careful about hiding them. Your wife only knows because she's been there when you've pulled your way gasping out of them in the dead of night.

You've been having them for a few years now but they seem to be getting worse. When your wife comforts you, tries to help you work out what might be causing them, you tell her you've no idea. That there's nothing in particular on your mind.

You're lying to her. But you tell yourself it's okay because it's to protect her. And your son.

Years ago, not long after you met her, you did a bad thing. A secret thing. Something you'll never tell anyone. Something that nobody else alive knows about.

You don't feel bad about it. You aren't a bad person, you know that. You did it to protect her, is how you square it with yourself. Although you're smart enough to know that that isn't the whole truth.

For years, you barely remembered the bad thing that you did. Hadn't considered it at all, until your dreams started getting more intense, started to grow details and develop context and make you think about the past.

But you don't let it bother you. They're only dreams and you're a practical guy. You aren't a bad person, and you did it to protect her, and your son. To protect your family.

The boy will grow out of it, you tell your wife and you tell yourself. Don't worry.

In a few weeks' time your wife will start to have bad dreams. Dreams of bindweed, creeping. There's a face in her dreams.

Why Why Not?

She rushes on ahead of him, the way she always does.

"Come on, it's up here!" she says.

He half-jogs to keep up. As he goes, he counts off bricks by pointing, and then reaches out and touches every fifth one along. He has done this for as long as he can remember when walking the wall, though he doesn't know when he started or why. Moving at speed makes this harder, and he appreciates the challenge.

There isn't much to break up the stability of life in City, and while that makes most people happy, distractions aren't unwelcome. Still, his feet are starting to hurt and he vaguely registers that she has been dragging him on through the outskirts for nearly an hour.

He stops and looks up at her, running on ahead. He's aware that to his left there are only fields and off in the distance, a mile or so away, a cluster of farm buildings and houses. They left City a while ago.

He leans against Wall, his hand against the most recent of the fifth bricks, his other hand removing the shoe from his lifted foot, shaking out tiny stones. Wall is there, solid and secure, from his hand and on. She is still running, getting smaller, and Wall runs alongside her. In the distance, way ahead of her, he can barely make out Wall's curve. He knows from trips to the lakes with his family that Wall continues on ahead of them describing that same curve, and from visiting his grandparents he knows that the circle continues way out on the other side of City behind them, too.

Wall is taller than most can crane their necks, but out here in the open he can see the top of it, where clouds cluster and push over. Wall is tall enough that when there are fires the smoke struggles to climb over it, drifting down the streets instead. Only the rarest breeds of bird ever migrate beyond the top of Wall.

"Are we close?" he shouts to her, before she gets out of range of his voice.

"We're here!" she calls back, and skips a few more paces before stopping and looking at Wall.

He has no idea what is so important that she couldn't just *tell* him, but he is relieved that they are finally there. He doesn't like surprises all that much but he likes her a *lot*, and she has always been one for adventures. He picks up the pace. Every fifth brick getting only the slightest scrape.

As he draws closer, he sees what she is so excited about. She is looking, rapt, through *a hole*! In *Wall*!

From the second he registers the absence of bricks he stops still, a ball in the pit of his stomach making him reluctant to move closer. Bricks lie in piles around the base of the hole where they have fallen. From here he can only see the clean grey of the exposed thickness of Wall, but can't see any further. From where she is standing, she must be able to see clearly into the hole, to where there is light that is shining on her face. The hole is tall, enough to drive a train through, but such is the vastness of Wall you wouldn't be able to see it from a distance.

"Come closer!" she says. "Come see!"

"Why?" he replies.

"Why?" she repeats. "Why not?"

"We might get into trouble," he says, and hates how weak he sounds.

"Why would we get into trouble?" she laughs. "There are no rules about this. Not that anybody ever told me, anyway. What about you?"

He quickly sorts through the rulebook in his head that catalogues every piece of advice – strict or informal – that he can remember ever being given. Lots of rules about eating and drinking. About tidying up and doing chores. And lots of laws about not hurting people or taking things. Mostly, things that seemed like common sense to him anyway.

But nothing about Wall. Wall is just there. Wall never changes. It hasn't ever really required any discussion or clarification. Wall is where Country finishes. It doesn't really occur to anybody to think outside of those parameters.

So, a hole in Wall is impossible for him to process. He feels oddly nauseous about the notion of there being an outside of Wall. He had thought they were *already* outside. He can't imagine how she could be brave enough to just stand there, in front of the hole, when he feels as if he is already too close. That he'll be sucked through.

"What… What can you see?" he asks, though he isn't sure he wants to hear the answer. "It's too complicated to explain!" Her infuriating reply. "Come see for yourself!"

He starts to step back as she starts to step forward, closer to the hole. There she is again, always pulling him on, dragging him behind her. That stab of irritation at himself returns. Life in City doesn't bring with it much sadness, but it has always made him insecure not knowing why she keeps his company.

He is thinking this when he stops moving backwards. Then he works out, maybe only a fraction of a second after she does, that she is about to step through the hole, to get closer to what she sees through there.

There isn't a fifth brick for him to reach out for. It is either at their feet or through the hole. So, he reaches out for her instead, and they go through together.

You Don't Know How It Starts; You Don't Know Where It Ends

His hands are deep in his pockets as they walk along the beach.

Pace: fast.
Mood: tense.

The sea and sand and sky give each of them an excuse to look somewhere other than each other.

Eyes: averted.

It's a beautiful day by the sea as they walk along, sometimes faster, sometimes slow. Every now and then he will say something that solicits a gasp of frustration from her that is harsher than the light breeze, and she will stride on ahead. He coils his fists deeper in his pockets when this happens, his shoulders hunching further down into his mood. It is as if his anger and anxiety are a black hole in the pit of his stomach, pulling everything in.

When this happens, they will walk on in silence for a few minutes.

She will brood in her way: All sudden turns and sharp twists.

He will brood in his: Slow to pick up speed and slower to change direction.

He will be staring out to sea, looking for reasons to be angrier and reasons to be calm. Either finding them or not in the distant hills and cliffs that look like they are on another island, but are actually just past the curve of shoreline, beyond where he can see.

Or at other times he'll see a cliff that he thinks is just along the way, just a distant part of where he is, and he'll be wrong: It's part of another country, distant across the sea.

While he is thinking about these things, she will always be staring ahead and deep inside. She will come to some conclusion, punctuated by fingers run quickly through her hair. A decision he won't see. She will stop, and let him catch up to her, and they'll walk side by side for a while, talk for a while.

Still arguing, but walking together at least.

Every now and then one of them will try to remember how this whole thing started, and whether or not their side in the row matters. They won't think to mention it, vaguely aware that it may weaken their place in the fight.

Every now and then the sun will set, and they soften. These will be the times when they stop together for a while, watch the night come on. Touch each other lovingly, acrimony forgotten.

Sink down into the sand and make love, as the air cools and the stars light up above them. As they lie there for a while, as their skin cools and their smiles light up, one or the other might ponder that of course, the stars were always there, and always as bright. You just can't see them for all the sun.

It will get cold, so they will walk the shoreline a while longer, moonlit and hand in hand. Until he, or she, or both, will say something or do something that recalls the row, and it will begin again.

At dawn, the light and warm and tide will soothe their tempers. She'll get hungry. He will buy her breakfast at one of the vendors on the beach front. Holidayers will start to appear, coming up to the beach from the hotels or resorts only a short way inland. Children will squeal and laugh as their parents lead them by the hand.

One of the couple might look off in that direction. They might consider leaving the beach. But the sun is high, and their bellies are full, and walking along by the water for a bit longer, trying to thrash this silly row out before rejoining the world, seems like a better idea.

After a while it is hard to tell where they walked on to the beach, or when. The coastline curves and curls, and the sandy beaches give way to pebbles, then to rocks, then back again. Neither remembers how big this island might be. Are they still exploring new ground, or have they gone around again?

The sea looks the same, beautiful and relentless wherever they walk to. There is no way to tell at the scale of a grain of sand or a pebble if it is one you've seen before. The distinction becomes redundant at a certain point.

Neither of them, if they stopped to question it, knows where this started. And neither of them knows how it will end.

They walk along the beach, his hands deep in his pockets.

It's a beautiful day by the sea. The sea and sand and sky give each of them an excuse to look somewhere other than each other.

Little Boxes

To hear my grandma tell it, giving birth to my dad was too easy. From before he was breathing air he was trying to run away. He pushed out into the world like he was trying to escape the womb.

Grandma told us a lot of stories about dad, after he'd left. She had a tendency to include details we didn't want to hear.

Dad's one defining characteristic was a desire to escape. He didn't like relying on people, didn't like to be relied on. Didn't like people caring about him, and didn't care himself. Didn't like feeling trapped.

Of course, that little thing didn't look like a thing, up to a certain point in his life. He left school and went to college. Left college and got a job. Left that job to get a better job. Met a woman, married her, bought a home, had kids.

From the outside he looked normal. To his family, he was a little simpler; a lot less normal.

His parents had expectations. Reasonable, but still they knew his name, and how they thought he should behave. He left them behind emotionally, as easy as he left her womb, and spent all his energy at school.

He found his horizons dwindling to a single narrow school corridor, and studied to escape, knowing that university was bigger, more open, more freedom to think and learn and play.

After three years of university he'd realised that education was limiting. Every stage of his life came down to being assessed and graded and fed back to about his progress, over and over, more expectation, more obligation, more requirement. His patience lasted only as long as it took to pass his course. Which was luck, not judgement.

He kept at his first job, but only because it wasn't challenging enough, and gave him so much freedom in his mind.

He ran away from solitude and into the arms of women. Fled the uncertainty of serial monogamy into a committed relationship with our mum. At some point the long nights got too restrictive and dull to him so he proposed to her; the logic being that for a few months they'd escape the claustrophobic silence and routines of their relationship, instead busying themselves with wedding arrangements.

The big day came and went, and as dad had guessed they spent the next several months talking about how it had gone, with all the attendant stories of friends and family getting too drunk and dancing to old disco.

Before long he felt trapped by those conversations and the routine of his life with mum and they decided to have kids. And that's where we came in. My sister and I.

And those early years were good. Dad was okay with us as toddlers. And he could change up who he was with us at that point because we were so young and our brains so plastic. Parents don't have to try hard to be funny or intelligent or themselves for little kids; we recognised his eyes and that he was our dad and he was immediately our hero, whatever mask he was wearing.

That changed when we started needing him to explain the world to us properly. When mum needed his help ferrying us from one place to the next. Suddenly our house was just another box that had formed around him; a giant existential trap.

He couldn't stay, so he went.

And that's when it changed for dad. His freedom splintered, split; at an existential level he started chasing one sort of freedom, always at the expense of the other.

He lived in a lovely large house for a while; smaller than our family home, but with more space for him. But the mortgage was punishing.

He ran away from the mortgage, so he was no longer locked into that for twenty years. But he was living in a smaller flat.

Around this time he finally realised that the working world was the worst - the most demanding - of all shackles, so he quit. He no longer had to work, total liberation. And routine was just another way that the world was telling him to stay in his box.

Before long he was leaving his flat in the morning to go and drink in the park, alone. And not long after that he was evicted from his flat, which he didn't mind so much because paying another person to live in a box went against everything he believed in.

At each stage he gained a personal freedom, while his options and horizons dwindled. For a while he was living on the street, swearing blind if you bumped into him that this was the life, that he'd never needed anyone before and no one could touch him. But he was wearing the same clothes for weeks at a time.

He decided to stop relying on the kindness of strangers to survive, feeling those particular tendrils of obligation moving in on him, and started taking from people instead. Started thieving and lying and cheating. The ultimate freedom; freedom from truth and from capitalism and a good day's work for a good day's pay.

Within six months he was in prison.

I visited him once there. He told me it was great. He wasn't expected to make any decisions, or talk to anyone, really.

His cell was the size of our toilet.

He started taking heroin while inside, we learned later. He ended his life addicted to it. I know exactly how that happened. The total freedom from responsibility of euphoria; the freedom from consequence from the inside of a hit.

But at that point, just before the end, his horizons had simmered down to a small black pinpoint around his soul, and he couldn't live a day without scoring.

At the end he didn't triumph over the cage of life victorious, even if that's how he might have explained it. He'd just run out of smaller rooms to escape into.

This is what I told Jane after the funeral. There on the hotel bed, me lying with my head in her lap.

"I hated him." I said, when I didn't know anything else about him to share. "He was a selfish prick. He didn't give us a second thought; we weren't people to him. Just another box he didn't want to end up dead in."

Jane's hands in my hair, soothing.

"I know, baby. I know," she said, calming.

We sat there quietly for a while.

Then something occurred to her.

"Is that why you had him buried, not cremated?" she asked.

I didn't reply.

Hemingway

At some point in the past I heard a story about Ernest Hemingway. At some point in the past, the story says, Hemingway wrote a six-word story for a bet.

"For sale: Baby shoes. Never worn."

That's the story that the story says Hemingway told. I think about this a lot. Probably too much. The recursive nature of it is in itself a miracle of the human experience.

Hemingway may never have told this story. This may just be an entirely fabricated thing – a story about Hemingway telling a story.

The fact that somebody can have lived less than fifteen years before I was born and there can be legends about them is sometimes still crazy to me. We will never know whether this thing didn't happen.

It's possible to prove to some extent that a thing like this did happen. A reliable written record - or a credible witness - is plenty for that. But it's almost impossible to prove the absence of something.

This is the snarled mess I can get myself in over a thing, and that's before even looking at the story within the story itself. Six words. Not enough for most people to form a viable thought in sentence form. But there's an undeniable narrative there, with an emotional snarl at the core of it that few could deny.

This time last year everything was worse. Things are better now, but the world is still more empty. Decades ago, when I was a child and lived in a different family, somebody else nearly happened. But can you prove it? It's almost impossible to prove the absence of something. Even when that absence sits in the middle of a family, and confronts you daily.

People might argue that six words can't be a story. Those people could say that Hemingway's maybe-tale is really just a statement. But if a story is a narrative spread like a virus from one person to others, then it is more than enough. I say you could shorten it further.

"Baby shoes"

Most of us see at least two stories there. One happy. One sad.

I've never been the sort of person who could lose a shoe in public. Perhaps that's why I can't walk past a discarded piece of clothing in the park or on the pavement, especially one that might seem as necessary as a sock or a dress or a shoe, without seeing a story in it. The story might be mundane. It's sometimes hilarious. But on occasion it is tragic.

We don't expect to see clothes without people. A dog with no owner begs questions. There will be some point in our life when we see an empty chair and it fills us with sudden and overwhelming sadness.

We tell ourselves stories about who we think we are. We tell ourselves stories about the people around us. When they're gone, they can't tell us any more stories that prove us right or wrong.

Hemingway wrote a six-word story for a bet. As far as I know, that's true.

That Is His Name, It Is Not Mine

I came to this place for sanctuary, and instead find myself in the thrall of a theological debate.

"I have told you, and know not how to tell you again, Father – these misshapen limbs and body are those of a man – one of God's own creatures – and I beg you to give me a place here to rest my lowly head."

"That you are a man is not in question, my son. It is your assertion that you are the son of the Doctor on the hill that cannot be ignored. And the lie you tell, that you were born to that man in absence of a wife."

I look beyond him into the dark and candlelight of the dry and warm cavern of worship there. I look back down at the old man, my eyes rheumy and wet. I wipe the mucus that gathers in lieu of real tears with the back of my hand.

"It is no lie, Father. Have you ever heard tell of a lady companion for the Doctor, down these long years? Or, indeed, of the echo of a child's laughter along those long and empty corridors? Look at me, with merciful eyes – could I have grown as a normal child to this great size without gathering the attention and rumours of the servants that come up and down from the village?"

He looks at me, a mixture of impatience and incredulity on his face.

"But what you say is an impossibility. And if it were not, it would be blasphemy! Man can not be born of man alone!"

I am young yet, but my life thus far has been hard, and has taught me much of irony and hypocrisy. I can not help an abrupt wave of my grotesque and massive hand, asking his attention back inside his church. I have not much experience of being loose around others, and I move too close to the old priest. His momentary recoil of fear makes me falter.

But my point is a valid one, and I make it again.

"Who decides such a thing? Look inside, Father. Look up there, above your altar. What of a man born of woman alone?"

"This is foolishness!" He exclaims, and moves back slightly into the shelter of his church, ready to close the door on this poor brutish fool. For that is yet how he sees me. "You test my patience, sir. It is only the Lord's mercy that stops me thrashing you soundly where you stand! Our blessed virgin mother Mary was visited upon by the spirit of the Lord. Would you have me believe that the Doctor was as well?"

He cannot help a sly laugh at that, but the smile soon leaves his face in the cold push and pull of the wind and rain.

I should go, and leave him to his peace. But it is so cold out here, the rain pouring down, the lightning flashing across the sky, and deep inside me something moves – the fluttering of the newborn's fear of the dark.

And father will soon realise that I am gone – soon there will be more to be scared of in the night than the lightning and the dark.

I go to my knees.

"Please, sir! I am telling you the truth. My father is a good God-fearing man, but he is also a servant of science. And science, to him, is also some sort of god. Science is the spirit that visited him, and aided in my conception."

"And, what? Should I think that you were grown from a seed like some twisted tree?"

"No, sir. My father, in the grip of his genius, found access to the remains of the dead. From that gruesome clay, he made me."

The priest grimaces, but then his face softens. God help me I think he may be pitying me, as he would a simpleton or some other manner of idiot.

"My son, do you believe that you were stitched together from the bodies of the passed? Did I make you out to be a charlatan when actually you are some poor, feeble-minded creature?"

"No. No sir. I am not lost in my own head. It is true. All of it."

I bow my head, so that I do not have to see his pity. My fingers rest in the wet dirt at his feet.

"I am born of my father's dreams. His dreams are great and terrible. But no more terrible or more great than those of any other parent, I am certain.

But his dreams are also beautiful and fragile, like clear-cut crystal or finest bone China, and I fear that holding them in these clumsy, brutish hands, they will be shattered."

I hold one hand out and up to the old man.

"And I was not stitched together like some poor girl's doll. I grew as any other child, in a bell-jar of vile and stinking liquid, the suspension fluid helping to form me out of the broken-down meat of the dead. Father saw that I grew fast, and without the nurturing of a female womb – see the smoothness of my skin…" And I forced my hand into his. "Like no man born of woman."

He folds his hands over mine – first curious, then frantic as he sees the truth of it. No marks on my skin. He pulls away the cloak that covers my naked flesh, and sees my body – as slick and smooth as my fingertips. No navel – in fact, no markings at all. I am fresh and new and hideous as father made me.

"What kind of unnatural creature are you?" He gasps, aghast.

"Not unnatural, Father. My creator is one of God's creatures. By natural law, that must surely make me one of God's creatures as well!" I cry. I feel the sting of rejection as he forces my hand violently away from his own fingers and retreats into the church.

I watch him go, and for an instant I force my eyes away from his judgement of me, look up at the ornate stonework above the church door. I had seen it from the path and thought it beautiful. Considered it a symbol of my shelter from the cruel rain.

Now it just looks like stone.

And I am still looking on it when the blow comes. Something sharp and harsh and metal against my heavy skull. The priest returned, with something – a weapon of some sort – from inside the house of God. I crash to the wet ground with my full weight, my arms going up to shield my head from the continuing blows. My face presses down into the sucking mud as I try to push myself forward, but my stupid addled brain – this takes me toward the entrance to the church, pushing past the attacking priest, where I will be trapped with whatever comes next.

Here, half inside the church and half out, there is no room for the priest in the doorway – he has to be content with raining blows down upon my legs and back. He cannot reach my shoulders any more, so I raise my head. I had been most afraid for my eyes.

From here I can see the altar clearly. From here I can look up at the large crucifix that towers over it; so large it would dwarf even me were I to stand beside it. From here I can see the salvation that I had believed so fervently in for what it is – the eyes looking down on me through tears of blood mark this out as a cathedral to nothing more than pain and sacrifice.

And though I had been pragmatic when bartering with the priest for entry, I can now see that the man on the cross and I are more alike than different. But he was followed before he was betrayed. He had a life. He was a leader of men, where I will ever be a pariah and a monster.

As I meet his eye as his equal, I choose to focus on the seemingly endless, monstrous pattern of assaults on my body. I choose to clench my fists beneath me. And I realise that what I am going to do next will be a choice, too – one that defines me.

I had hoped to leave my father's home and find my place among other men, but I realise now that I am not a man. I am something else and something more.

And I am damned if I will let them crucify me before I've had my time.

Moments later, I look at what I have done. It won't be long before the local folk find the remains of their priest, and then they will be coming for me, with my father the Doctor close behind.

Let them.

With Flaming Locks Of Auburn Hair

The showgirl's body was still cooling when Watson arrived in the modest rooms where she died. The sheriff was looking down at the body and bare nodded his head on the smaller man's arrival.

"Argus." he said.

"Jared." Watson responded. "So, who is the lady?"

"She's a dancer at the Ruby. Lady J, her name was."

"Hmm." Watson said, taking off his hat and holding it in one hand. "Hmm." he said again, walking around the body. "Pretty lass."

"The prettiest in town, some reckon. There's a few fellas who'll be sorry she's gone."

"Hm. She's been shot, then? Little hole just here…" Watson indicated an entry wound just under the woman's chin. He lifted the head, fingers gentle and slow and careful like a lover as they found purchase amid the dark and deep red hair. "…And a much bigger one here." he said, nodding down at the back of the head for the benefit of his audience.

The deputy, standing quiet up till now, leaned in to the sheriff and stage-whispered, "Jesus, we need a Pinkerton to tell us that?"

Watson stopped moving about the body for a moment, but didn't look up.

"Remind the deputy to mind himself, Jared." he said, and before the man could react, continued, "And that I'm a Pinkerton no longer."

The deputy settled back on his heels and smouldered, but had the sense to stay quiet. The sheriff couldn't help but smile a little. He looked out of the hotel window, down on the mud and bluster of the street.

Before long Watson spoke, breaking the sheriff out of his reverie.

"You said that there would be men that missed her?"

"Certainly did, Argus. A few as visited with her. But I don't see none of 'em doing her in." He looked away from the window, and winked at his friend. "The lady got what she wanted from 'em, 'n they got what they needed from her, 'n all seemed right happy with the arrangement."

"She doesn't look like a whore."

"Certain she doesn't, 'n she ain't. She was a classy lady." The sheriff pulled a pipe out of his shirt pocket, examined it. "But had a way about her with the fellas, 'n the sense to make use of her God-gived talents."

After a few more moments, the sheriff asked if the detective was satisfied. He nodded yes, and the sheriff moved to his deputy.

"Tell Dearborne that he can come clear her out." he told him, and his subordinate left the room. He turned back to wink again at Watson. "Old cocksucker'll be having a fit, thinkin' about this room sittin' here earning nothin' but flies."

Watson managed a small and cautious smile.

"Do you think, Jared…" he said, pausing for a moment as he looked back down at the once beautiful woman. "Do you think you might furnish me with a list of those men?"

* * *

Watson, Sheriff Jones and Deputy Wolcott arrived at the Gantry farm around midday, less than two hours after Lady J bore scrutiny for the final time. It was noon.

Jim Gantry saw them coming from a ways off, and made his way back from the field to greet them on his porch.

"Jared," he noted, as if checking the name off. He nodded to the deputy. "Bill." He looked at the small man in the tidy suit and hat. "And who is this?"

"This is Mr Argus Watson, Jim." the sheriff said, as he took Gantry's hand in a firm handshake. "He's helping me out with some matters about town."

"About town?" Gantry said, and then, catching something in the sheriff's voice, looking from man to man: "What's this about, Jared?"

* * *

"Ella!" he called, and then louder, "ELLA!"

"What is it, James?" his wife asked as she rushed into the room, drying her hands on a rag. She stopped short when she saw the three unexpected men sitting at the table. She turned instantly to her husband and said "Has something happened in the town?"

Gantry looked blankly at his wife as he stood, his hand on the back of a chair as if he were about to pull it out for her. He didn't move, though.

Watson broke the silence, which made the woman start.

"We're sorry for the imposition, ma'am." he said, meeting her eyes as she spun to look at him. He kept his tone reassuring, and his eyes were kind.

She was a small, delicate woman, pretty in her way. Even worried as she was she had a sweetness in the eyes. Watson tried to imagine that she didn't remind him of his *own* wife, these five years dead.

"There's been a tragedy in town." he said. The lady's eyes widened.

"What sort of tragedy?" she said.

"A murder, ma'am. Of a showgirl."

Ella Gantry's hands went to her mouth, and she slumped into one of the dining chairs, facing the visitors.

"Oh, that's just terrible." she said. After a few moments she lowered her hands, folding them one over the other in front of her on the table top. "But why are you here?"

Watson turned first to the sheriff, and then to the deputy – both men turned away, suddenly shy, unable to meet Mrs Gantry's eye.

"Well, you see… Hmm. The lady was known to have the occasional dalliance with one man or another around the town."

She looked at him blankly. Watson went on.

"And I'm afraid that one of her gentlemen was Mr Gantry."

Ella Gantry turned suddenly to glare up at her husband. For his part, Jim Gantry seemed oblivious to the events unfolding in the room. He was staring somewhere else, into another room. In that other room, lit by candlelight, lay another woman.

Mrs Gantry looked back at Watson, the new focus of her anger.

"And you think my James did it?" she said. She laughed – an unhappy sound at odds with her previous softness. "That he's an adulterer is slim surprise, but a killer? Look at him… the man's a farmer to his belly. He…" Her voice cracked. "… He couldn't hurt a fly, out of spite."

Watson was used to the stillness that filled the room, then. A moment, maybe two, when he could step away from this; leave the guilty to move on with their guilt, take the easy road. In a moment there would be pain. One way or another there always was.

But the man who knows right from wrong should always go forward with right. That was something he had always believed before, and he felt that his poor wife's spirit would look on him with sadness if he admitted his doubts now.

The silence had rushed in to fill the space left by Mrs Gantry's words. Watson spoke into it.

"We know that, Mrs Gantry. We know that Jim didn't kill Lady J," she looked relieved.

"Well, good." she flustered. "I knew he couldn't. It must have been one of her *other* men."

"If it were that would be easier, ma'am. A man, when he kills – it's generally a thing of anger or just plain meanness. It is easy to deal with a man, because once he kills the once, he's a killer throughout." Watson put his hands down flat on the table in front of him. He looked suddenly older.

"I've seen men take an innocent life by accident, and turn animal almost on the spot. Hanging a man who kills, that's almost like a mercy killing."

The sheriff and deputy kept their eyes on fixed spots, everywhere but on the conversation at the table.

"But the thing is, the dead girl, the hole in her, it was small. It didn't come from any gun that a man'd be carrying. It was a woman's pistol."

"So? I don't understand. Another showgirl shot her?"

"That's a possibility, yes. Except that, you see, the lady, in costume as she was when she was murdered, stood almost as tall as your husband there. And the… I beg your pardon, but… the mess that left her body from the wound was high on the wall, as if she had been standing." The lady put a hand to her mouth again, this time in disgust. She looked away, as if Watson's words were a picture and she could hide from it.

"Why are you telling me this?" she said.

"Because the dead woman, the bullet entered through her chin, but the wound it made as it left her was high up, up here, on the back of her head." Watson said, straining slightly as he indicated the spot on his own scalp. "You see Lady J was standing tall, and to create such a wound her murderer would have to have been standing shorter than her. By about a head and a half."

"This is insane." Mrs Gantry cried, and stood up suddenly from her chair, the noise of it against the planks of the floor shocking the three previously absent men back into the conversation. "You can't possibly know the things that you are saying."

"I assure you, I can, ma'am. And more, I can tell you that of all the poor women who suffered for the lack of the money and attention that their men paid to the lady, you are the only one of a more… petite stature."

The farmer's wife began to respond, denial on her face. Then she seemed to crumple, falling back into the chair, suddenly even smaller.

"You're right." she said.

"I know." said Watson. The sheriff and his deputy got up from their seats quietly on either side of him. Jim Gantry had taken two silent steps back away from his wife, and was now just staring at her aghast.

"I didn't mean to. I didn't mean to kill the girl."

"I know, Mrs Gantry. I believe you."

"I just…" the woman started to sob, great wet groans that belied her size. "I just went there to see her. To tell her to leave my man be."

Watson fished a 'kerchief out of a pocket, and passed it across the table to her. She dabbed it at her eyes absently, not really in the room – in fact, in the same room that her husband had been staring into earlier.

"But when I saw her… and she was so beautiful. I knew I couldn't compare to her, and that I'd lose him to her for sure. So, I begged her, I begged her not to take my James from me. But she looked back at me, and it was like she didn't even see me."

"And that is when you shot her." Watson stated.

"… Yes. It was her gun. It was just lying there, in among her trinkets on the side. It made a popping sound, and then she wasn't there any more… she was down there on the floor. And I just stood still, waiting to be struck down. I waited for someone to come and find me. But nobody did. Not then, and not afterwards, as I left the hotel."

Ella Gantry raised her head from her hands, face red with tears, and looked at Watson, a half-formed question in her eyes.

"I thought I'd dreamed it." she said.

"You didn't." Watson said. He stood up from his chair and moved toward the kitchen, allowing the lawmen space to take the woman into custody. "I'm sorry." he muttered, but by then nobody was listening.

Adventures Underground

The alleyway presents itself, which seems like an odd thing for an alleyway to do but there it is, and here I am. I stop on my own tracks and examine my situation, scratching my head.

I like the way the back of my head feels and for a second I forget where I am, rubbing my fingers through the short-short hair down to the nape of my neck, almost purring with the feeling.

My dad used to have these big books, proper comic books. They were in French and I couldn't read them but there was this kid in them with a little white dog, and I always loved his hair.

Before I even knew what my bits were for I got a strange tingle, thinking what that boy's head might feel like, all fuzzy and flat, with the long bit out front for tugging onto.

Got the 'do' done for myself when the time seemed right. And I love it. But not as much as my BF does. And he does know what my bits are for. Alright, he's never on time, but I proper love him.

That brings me back to my present predicament, thinking of my BF heading for home, him fretting, thinking about me. Thinking that I'll be waiting for him, ready to go at it like rabbits.

But I've got to get these last few errands done, and then there's the alleyway, you see. I didn't see it coming but here it is, and I'm wondering if my hurry is worth risking it.

You try, if you've got your head still about you, to avoid enclosed spaces hereabouts. If you want to be clear on where you're going you make sure that you can always see where you've been.

Because most of the time when you go through a door here, you can't be sure of where you'll end up. And if you can't see where you've been, you can't be sure of getting back there again.

This means that alleyways are to be mistrusted. Going indoors is okay, but never let a door close behind you if you can help it. Keep an eye on windows. It's one of the rules to live by.

But I do love that boy, and besides nothing all that bad ever happens here, even if you do get lost. Not much frightens you after a few years of travelling around, not even the Red Queen's men.

So, there's this alleyway and it's between where I am and where I want to go, or at least it seems to be. So, I figure what the hell and in I go with only the odd glance behind me.

And it's all going well enough, the alleyway only changing a little bit and behind me staying the same all along, until the outside walls and windows seem to give way to rock, and then to wallpaper.

Cobblestones becoming dirt, becoming more like lino, black and white tiles like in my parents' bathroom. I gulp down the same old feeling of disquiet, thinking:

Oh, fuck. Another adventure.

Looking behind, I realise that I've lost track of my trail. I'm not where I was. I'm all inside, now. And there's these mirrors, a whole corridor of mirrors, like in that film with Bruce Lee.

I keep moving past a hundred reflections of me. Most of them look the same or similar, fashionably torn fishnets, spunky forelock all for tugging, big belt, leather jacket a bit worn from scurrying down holes.

Now and then there's another, though, looking similar but not the same, looking back at me, or just not noticing. There's this one, she barely looks like me at all. Looks like *ye olde me*, in a world of her own.

After a while of walking, and this other girl recurring in the mirrors, all posh and ancient in her blue and white whatever-the-fuck sort of clothes those are, I start to take more notice of her.

Then I stop moving all together, and she kind of does too, but a few seconds after me. I look at her, she looks back. I move my hand, she copies the movement, a mirror image. Annoyed, she wrinkles her nose.

I wrinkle my nose too. I move toward the mirror and she does the same, matching my timing perfectly. I think on it, decide that I will surprise her, thinking that I will reach out quick, pinch her nose.

Suddenly she reaches out and pinches my nose. I yelp and jump back, my arm instinctively going out and boxing her on the shoulder. The shock makes her let go of my face, and I yell at her.

"What the fucking hell do you think you're doing, mush?" I say.

"I beg your pardon?" she says, sounding much older and posher than either of us. I rub my sore nose and scowl at her.

"I said why'd you do that for?" She thinks about it for a moment.

"Well, I suppose that I thought that you were a reflection of me. That is, after all, how a looking-glass would normally behave."

"Does this place look normal to you?" I say, and she looks around. I do the same. We're in a cave now, no mirror in sight.

"Well," she says, "this *is* a day for surprises."

"Surprises? It's a fucking abortion of a day!" I say, and head for daylight. She hangs on for a second, wondering whether I'm worth the risk, and then follows me closely through the earth.

"I am in the same predicament as you. There is no need to be so... truculent," she says.

"Like I know what *'truculent'* means!" I gasp.

"I hardly see how your ignorance is my fault," she says. "I suppose that is the difference between a lady and a child. The former might ask to be enlightened, while the latter might take comfort in oblivion."

She keeps twittering on but to be honest by this point I'm starting to tune her out. We're not in the cave any more, for what that's worth. Now we're in the woods.

That's worse.

She stops talking when she hears the low growling coming from out where we can't see. I reach into my pocket and pull out my weapon.

Even as I unsheathe the tiny blade, I hope to fuck that I don't have to use it. My tiny Vorpal flick-knife is hardly going to be any good against a fucking Jabberwock.

I signal her to keep quiet, but it's more for the peace than anything else. I've already pegged her as being a lot like one of the clever bitches back at the boarding school. I can't be arsed.

I reach into the side-pocket of my rucksack and thumb my phone on. My fucking luck, there's no signal, though, is there? Little girl lost looks at the thing, and I remember that she's not from round here.

But then, neither am I. It's my 'back home' that she's not from. And I'd be lost in her part of town, too.

It's my time she's foreign to. Time works different here.

I'm guessing they didn't even have Beyonce back in her day. Bloody cavemen.

Wonder what they did about periods? You can't get tampons in Wonderland, like you can't get most other things. I end up carrying loads in my bag.

You know, just in case.

The growling doesn't stop but doesn't get any closer either, and she only bloody starts moving out towards it, eyes wide and curious. I'm tempted to let her get fucking et.

But the thing is, you can't get anywhere without going somewhere first and at least she's got the right idea there, so I let the clueless cow go on ahead and I follow a few steps behind.

And as we get closer it's more obvious that the roaring isn't growling at all; it's got a rhythm to it. It's fairly clear even before we're in the clearing that what we're hearing is actually snoring.

Once we're in the clear, the clearing doesn't look much like a clearing at all. The trees are so close together that it's more like the inside of a log cabin. The floor is perfectly mowed grass.

Except for in the shadow of the large picnic table in the middle of the space, where instead there's only wood panelling. The table top is also covered in grass, but here it has grown wild.

Flattening down the blades of grass are dinner plates, laid out around the edges of the table as if for absent eaters. Serving platters of food are piled high around the table's centrepiece.

A veggie's nightmare, platefuls of sausages, pies and pepperoni pizza, as well as large bowls of Skittles, M&Ms, other stuff I don't recognise. Chips, and gravy, and veg, but no sprouts.

And in the middle, lying flat on his back, mouth half-open as the wettest snoring I've ever heard bellows out of him, is the Red King. It doesn't seem the smartest thing, sleeping in the grass. I say so.

"Shhh," the other girl says. "You might wake him."

"So?" I say, and realise that I don't really care how she answers. She answers anyway.

"He might be dreaming, and you could give him a terrible fright."

I get what she's saying. Where there's a King, there's a Queen, and the Red one is the *worst* one. Thinking about it now, my fella has *told* me about the sleeping King, out here in the woods.

About how he used to be about the only thing keeping the old bitch in check, and how nobody quite knows how he went to sleep, and why he never wakes up.

"They used to be the King and Queen of Hearts, you know," I whisper. "Now it's just the Reds."

"What do you suppose happened to the Diamonds?" she replies. I don't know, but don't admit it.

"My bloke says that when this bloke wakes up, things will be different," I say. "But the thing about this place, it's *always* different already."

She ponders that, then moves closer to the King, prodding him.

"I *had* thought that I *might* be dreaming all this," she says, sliding his eyelid open, looking into his flat wet eye. She tuts. "Perhaps it is *him* that is dreaming *us*."

"Not the weirdest thing I've ever heard," I say, searching for an exit. "Best stop poking him then." That makes sense to her. She glances around the room.

"I remember this place," she says. "I believe that I have been here before. Or perhaps, is it possible, might I be remembering that I will be here at some time later on?"

"That would be pre-membering," I correct her. My tummy makes a growling sound of its own, and I glance at the food. She follows my look, and I hear the sound echo in her own belly.

"Why, I feel as if I haven't eaten since tea-time," she says, more to the room than to me. I'm almost used to these free-roaming exclamations, so I only notice her reaching out for a cake…

… once she's already taken a bite out of it.

"No!" I shout. "You stupid bitch. Don't eat anything that's been left lying around. No eating, no drinking. It's one of the fucking rules!"

But of course, she's already gone.

And that isn't even surprising any more. If it isn't shrinking, it's growing so long and thin that people can't even see you.

If it isn't falling asleep for a hundred years, it's suddenly bouncing a thousand miles at a time. If it isn't becoming so fast that you can't be spotted by the naked eye, it's becoming actual full-on invisible.

At which point it's irrelevant, isn't it? You're on the next page, moving onto the next chapter, and you're lucky if you see that last room again. S'like life is a series of weird little escapades. All very odd.

Over the snoring I can suddenly hear footsteps, loads of them, and I remember about the Red Queen, the creepy old cow, watching over Wonderland, claiming heads left, right, and centre.

I'm guessing that she doesn't really want people bothering her old man here, and I start looking more frantically around for a way out. I hadn't noticed the door, but then suddenly there's a banging at it.

Just like the police back home, three hard bangs and then the shouting of a young male soldier, nervous with borrowed authority, worth fuck all. Just a bunch of pawns, as it goes.

I glance at the King but he's still sleeping, doesn't even murmur.

"Let us in, on the Red Queen's authority!" Soldier One shouts.

Hard core pawn, I grin, to and despite myself.

Full of hectic energy I look harder for a way out, and then I look up and notice the window in the ceiling. I guess that was where the light came from, as it seems to look out onto a sunny meadow.

Of course, that doesn't make any sense, but what does, anyway?

When I first came here, I'd have thought that the window was out of reach, but now I'm not green anymore and I know different.

All it takes, if I can ignore the sounds of shouting, battering and straining wood for a minute, is to concentrate on what it would be like if this room were to just roll on its side, so I could walk on the wall.

And so, of course, I can do exactly that. The world spins on its axis. The wooden slats of the wall are hard under my feet, and I have to reach to push the window open, but then, with just the slightest bit of dizziness, I'm through.

The sun is warm on my skin. I can hear the final splintering of the door being smashed out of its frame, and the shouting of young men, so I look behind me to see an oak tree, a hollow knot in its side.

Looking into the knot, there's that disorientation again as I'm looking down into the darker room, with the sun still on my back. The soldiers seemed scary before, but now they look so small and silly.

"Hey!" I shout, getting their attention. They all look up at me at once.

"Stop," they shout, and "thief!" And I'm wondering what they're on about, but then I look down at the table and see that it's bare.

Then, of course, I notice that there's something in my hand. I don't even need to look at it to know that it's a chess piece… after a while, you get a feel for the way that this place works.

I grin, thinking about how my bloke will react when he sees what I've managed to find for him. Half-horrified, half-gleeful, I reckon.

He used to work for big Red. She wasn't very nice to him.

I wonder about the annoying girl and where she might end up.

I wonder what uses a once loyal white rabbit might find for a sleeping monarch.

"The Queen will have your head!" the soldiers shout, but what they really mean is if they go back empty-handed, she'll have theirs.

Silly fuckers.

I wonder what else is waiting for me before I find my bed.

I turn from the tree and walk into the brightening day, ignoring the raised voices.

"Who cares for you?" I mutter at the frustrated soldiers and their bitch Queen. "You're nothing but a pack of bastards."

The Wire Jumpers

I look up into the dark blue evening through my own misting breath, and sigh. I listen to the humming up above us.

"So, what am I looking at?"

"It's a power line." says Joe Malone, my childhood friend, lost all these long, lonely years. He's back on the scene in the months since Jody left for Oz.

"Right. You see, I *thought* that was what it was. At least I haven't *totally* lost it."

"It's where the power goes?" he says, confirming that we are both on the same page. We aren't. I am too distracted by the lack of feeling in my toes. I look down at him. He seems shorter than I remember.

"Riiight. Great. Well, this should help me get to Jody."

I have come a long way in the years since Joe and I first played together. I have discovered sarcasm. My world is much richer for it, *obviously*.

"Well, yes, it should." he says, not quite understanding my tone.

I look around, searching the field for anything like a pub. I am out of luck it seems, although I do see the alarming shadows of some horses drifting large and haughty in the gloom nearby.

I have somewhere elses to be, and other things on my mind than hanging around in the cold with someone who may or may not be a bit not-quite-right. I'd be angry at anyone else for the massive time-suck this evening is becoming, but a look at Joe's big, happy eyes, full up of worry and pity in a way that they never were for the eight-year-old version of me, takes the wind right out of my sails, and a good deal of the vinegar out of my mood.

I'm still full of piss, and may need to do something about that in a bit, but I keep quiet about it. Checking the ground around me as best I can for cow shit, I slump down on the damp earth.

"I don't see how it can help, Joe. It's just a wire. Maybe if it was a phone line, I could call her, but…"

"You said that if you looked your friend in the eye, and finally told her how you really felt, she wouldn't have to marry that man she met, and you could both finally have what you really wanted."

"I don't think that's exactly how I put it." It sounded quite naive, put like that. "Besides, how does this have anything to do with that? Australia is, like, a million miles away. And I don't think she'll change her life on the strength of a phone call from a bloke who's flaked out on her as many times as I have. And…" I add, somewhat feebly, "… It's really bloody cold out here!"

"So, look her in the eye." He winks at me, but to tell the truth, it might just be him squinting against the moon, the angle he's at.

"How?"

"Don't you remember how it used to be?"

The first time I met him, I was an eight-year-old lad who might or might not have just wet himself. My main enduring memory of the event was that I was crying, and was embarrassed that anyone might see me with snot and tears running down my face. Luckily, the reason I was crying was that the boys who had pushed me down the hill had had no interest in sticking around to keep me company, and as such I was all alone. So that had worked out okay.

Still, I sat there, sobbing my nose out. There's a way of crying that you don't tend to do once you've grown up a little, where your body shakes as if it is trying to throw the tears out of your little face, like some sort of Ebola of sorrow. It is *not* pretty. And it meant that I didn't notice Joe until he was *right there* in front of me.

"Hello. Do you want to play?" said the strange little man. Although of course he didn't seem so little to me back then.

I had rubbed the collected tears and snot off my face, shy again, and had looked him up and down. To be honest I can't really remember much about what I saw, now. I *was* eight, after all.

"Mum says I'm not allowed to talk to strangers." I sniffled.

"Well, then. What is your name?"

"I'm Joseph. Joe."

"That, young man, is an incredible coincidence... I too am Joe. Joe Malone, the World Hopper. And you and I are no longer strangers. So, shall we play?"

Of course, now I realise how desperately dodgy that all sounds, but it was the beginning of the most incredible friendship, packed with incident and excitement, every day full of the promise of strange people and exotic lands. The details of which are admittedly hazy to me now, as I guess most people's memories of the time before they crashed headlong into the wonderful world of puberty are.

Still, when he asks me if I remember it all, I can't help but get an inkling of the magical. I get the strangest sense of having been in a different amazing place every day, and wonder how peculiar it is that an eight-year-old could have imagined such things.

I look at him, and make a dumb noise that indicates that I might or might not recall what he's on about, and I might or might not feel some way or another about it.

It is almost identical, I realise, to the sound I made whenever Jody brought up the subject of she and I being maybe more than just friends. My cheeks go red and my forehead burns.

But again, that might be the cold.

Joe Malone takes it as a signal to keep talking.

"So… Earlier today we were talking about power lines?"

"Well, yeah, we were. But I thought you meant, you know, ley lines or something like that. I mean, that seemed to be what you were getting at… Not pylons."

"Power is power, Joe. There are lots of different ways to get to where you want to go, if you don't go wanting to see things like power as lots of *different* things."

"Okay. Right. I'm pretty sure most of what you just said doesn't mean anything."

"Well, that's as maybe. But so is this: the distance between you and your girl is a million miles, and at the same time it's a heartbeat. If you picked up the phone and spoke to her the distance would be the width of that humming noise coming from up above us."

"Hm. Did this stuff ever make any sense to me when I was a kid?"

"To be honest, Joe, no, not really. You used to make that same dumb face that you are making now. But, okay, maybe I shouldn't try and explain. Maybe I should just show you. Take my hand?"

And he offers me a pick me up, pulling me from my muddy seat. And then somehow we're perched way up high on a wire, and I can look down and see the horses and the field below. And suddenly it all comes back to me.

"Oh, hang on a minute… I just remembered why you were called Joe Malone, the World Hopper."

I try not to let it occur to me that I am standing atop a humming filament only an inch or two across, and I do a fairly good job of it all things considered. Because my mind is full of a thousand bright adventures, and I have realised that I really will soon be seeing Jody, and everything will be alright.

"We used to go all over the shop… every country under the sun, and some that were under *other* suns. And you always found a different way to take us there."

He grins at me, and I know that it is just my new grin reflected back.

"Actually, I was called Joe Malone because that's *your* name. But you are right about the rest. Except the journeys were only different in some ways. In another way, they were always the same. We always left from point 'a'. And we always ended up at point 'b'!"

And then he winked, and the wire beneath our feet started to vibrate more than before, faster and faster.

"Joe Malone, you are right." I say to him. "Shall we be off?"

"Right you are, Joe Malone!" He winks again. And the cold, dark, blue night blinks away around us.

And then we *are* off; Joe Malone and Joe Malone, off on their latest greatest adventure.

At Home In The Crumple Zone

It takes a polite but firm question at the bar to find out that he's in the back room. It only takes a particular kind of look to get security to let me by.

I take the seat opposite him. It's so rare that anyone disturbs him back here that he doesn't even notice me until I'm fully settled. I'm smiling as he looks up, and I'm smiling when his eyes widen.

To his credit, he's got it under control again almost instantly.

"Serene," he says, using the name I gave him, greeting me like we had a poker game scheduled or something.

"Mr Jacobs."

"What can I do for you?" he asks, quietly folding the paper he was reading and putting it to one side.

He's probably confident enough not to have a gun on him in here. He's definitely smart enough not to try and use one on me.

There's no useful way to answer his question, so I ignore it.

"I've had an interesting time with cars in the past, you know." I say instead.

He says nothing.

"I remember in '93, back in Britain: I was going too fast on a too slow road, and the car spun out hard. Can't remember when the air-bag engaged, but it was quite a thrill, really. The impact hurt a little, but the other cars I hit came off worse."

He grunts.

"Air-bags, you see? Air-bags were kind of a revelation for me. I went a bit out of control in the '90s, after that first time. Probably totalled around ten or eleven cars in '95 alone, just off the back of adrenaline driving. I don't take a lot of care usually anyway, but impact without pain and injury? I wanted some of that.

Course, sometimes tough to get a feel for a stolen car, so there were times there where I came off that little bit worse – not every car had the bags, and in a hurry you couldn't always tell. Some hairy old times, I have to tell you. One time, I went through a windscreen and under a Volkswagen van. It took hours under the knife before I was a shape that the nurses could look at without freaking out.

But that's just stupid macho driving, isn't it? It's a bit embarrassing to talk about it now, really…

this was before I went professional, and my life required more… finesse."

He is staring at a point on my face. It's hard to say whether that's nerves, or just that there's something on my face. Did I shave this morning, I wonder? Hm. It probably actually is just nerves. He knows why I'm here.

"Over the years, I've lived through, what, four… maybe five drive-by shootings? I don't know if you can count those, but I *was* in cars at the time, so I guess you can. All here in the US, of course.

What *is* it with this country, murder and cars? Aside from that car-bomb in Ireland, every time someone's tried to off me either *in* a car or *with* a car, it's been here. I know it's a big country and all, and I shouldn't judge the whole place by a few incidents, but seriously!

So, anyway, what, shootings, crashes… and a couple of times I've been run down, but one of those was Italy and I'm not entirely sure that wasn't just an accident, the way they drive.

Oh, and then of course there's the movie-villain telegraphed killings. The chloroform-and-leave-in-peril gambit. You'd be surprised at how many people try that on.

Well, maybe *you* wouldn't.

Some nice touches there, by the way. Not sure how much you leave to the initiative of your guys, but most people wouldn't bother with the bullets, restraints, trunk *and* river dump combo. Your guys are thorough."

His expression doesn't change, but he quickly moves to stand up. I raise my index finger. I'm not sure what the signal is supposed to mean, but Colombo used to do it all the time and it seems to work. He sits back down sharp.

"That's right," I say, "stay calm. Don't worry, nothing really very bad is going to happen here. I'm just going to wait until you open up that laptop and I get paid for the work I did for you. I'm not in the habit of disposing of paying customers. This little chat is just to remind you that it's polite to *pay* for services rendered."

I sit and wait while he taps at the keyboard. I'll make sure, of course, but the furtive glances he keeps flashing at me tell me that he's unlikely to try and rip me off – or kill me – again. At least till his sphincters relax a little.

He's looking at that same spot on my face. I reach up to it and give an exploratory rub. A large dark fleck falls away and lands in front of me on the table, and I wonder if maybe I should have showered before I came. I brush a few similar flecks from the collar of my shirt. They all land in a small pile on the table, which I scoop onto the floor with the back of my hand.

After not very long he closes the laptop, and pushes it to one side. Seconds later my cellphone buzzes with a text from my accountant confirming the transaction.

He says nothing as I stand to go. At the door I think of something and turn back to him, and this time he doesn't have the composure to hide his fear.

"You know," I say, "the *first* time I died in a car was my first time dying full-stop. Back then the cars weren't so fast, but if you dropped one down a hillside, it'd crumple up around you quicker than a pocketed fifty on a street corner.

I did it to myself, mind. Kind of expected it to be final, but it didn't take. And here we are today…"

I let that sit in the air, and leave him to it.

A Pretty Steep Learning Curve

You rest your hand on the wing. Cold metal under your fingers, tiny droplets of water, out here near the tip.

Big, commercial passenger jets may be easiest to find, but they are also the most risky. There are always plenty of furtive eyes in the cabin excitedly looking out at the view, or nervously checking for flaws in the wing.

Best if nobody sees you out here, even if it's likely that nobody would believe them anyway.

Risky, sure, but so satisfying. So large and fast and unlikely, and even just a touch makes you feel like you're a part of that… as if you're somehow helping keep it up.

It's pretty cold up here.

Nobody ever talks about that in the comics or movies. Invulnerable doesn't mean impervious, and you can feel the cold the same way you'd feel the heat of a fire. It hurts, it just doesn't *damage* you.

But as you and the jet fly into a cloud, you know the cold is worth it.

The thing is, this isn't actually that easy. For a start you have to match speed with the plane *exactly*, which isn't as intuitive as it might sound. And you can't just swoop in and put your hands on a bird like this out of a clear blue sky. Alongside it like this it might seem like a tiny thing like you could only be insignificant next to such a relentless, huge machine, but the different parts of these birds operate in a delicate state of equilibrium when in flight. The shape of it shifts, parts moving against and around each other in an incredible feat of engineering that all happens around oblivious passengers.

The slightest misjudging of trajectory, or a little bit too much pressure or drag on the wrong part of an engine or fin or panelling, and you could rip a wing clean off. You could flip the whole bird off its axis or into a spin. Moving too slow or too fast toward a thinly skinned metal tube moving at almost 900 miles per hour you could tear a hole in the hull or tear the bird in half without even trying. Plane and passengers, raining to the ground, and only you ever knowing you were there.

It took you a while to get the hang of it. But you know that it was worth it.

As Every Father Did

My father was the greatest of us and when life finally brought him low, as it does us all, it was my sacred task as his youngest son to lay him to rest.

With two wives and goodness knows how many other men and women, the hard work of several lifetimes, many children and more grandchildren…

With more than a few dozen battles, in more than a couple of wars…

It was still no surprise that it was his heart that did for him… It was just too big.

Too full of those women, those children, all of those fallen comrades and other comrades besides still taking a swig at the bar.

So, I carried his meat and his bones as is tradition, over one of my too weak shoulders, to the chosen place, the place chosen out for his best fitted memorial.

And I rested his carcass down on the soft earth before the bare, flat, rock sheet that stretched on as far as the eye took you.

And I set to work, at first slowly, but gaining speed with every exertion.

This is how I did it.

I chose my spot in the rock. And I flexed my slender craftsman's fingers, and tested my tapered, craftsman's hands. I touched the spot in the rock that I had chosen. I drew back my hand into a fist. And uncoiled it at the rock, as a scorpion's tail.

The first cut ached in my mind as it always does, as my mind always did, recoiling at the impact of extended fingers on rock before remembering that this caused me no pain; that my hands glide through rock, as steel through sinew, or a storyteller's breath through a lie.

Because father was born a Warrior, and a Man, and a Father, but I was only born a Builder. Simply a Stone Shifter. And this is what I do.

So, I scooped out giant boulders of rock, one a hand, and tossed them to one side, shoulders strengthening with each throw, until I had hollowed out a place in the permanence of stone for my father. I lifted him into it. I said the words. I tried to remember him as best I could in that single moment, as clearly as my simple, Stone Shifter's heart would let me.

And I buried him. Returning the stone, with him beneath. Rock on boulder on bone. Until all the stones were returned, and his heart underneath pushed them into a mound.

And then I kept on, tearing up fresh rock, gouging pools and then valleys in the steady, ancient face that nothing had previously marked, not allowing the tears in my eyes out onto my face, building and building, making a hill of my father, always so steady, always so sure. Making a mountain of him, his shadow always reaching out, his silhouette never far from the horizon.

For days I tore at the world, building fitting tribute to my father; weeks, until I had nothing left to give. And then I fell, and slept for a year, hands reaching out, a weakness in our world, hands reaching out to the mountain now where my father stood before.

When I woke, the grass had grown around me. A year of inertia and entropy and the natural world on my skin. The mountain stood.

There are others that I have built, now. Other mountains, other memories. For every thing that I have built with intention, I have devastated lives and torn canyons out of the world through lack of care. But in my father's memory I try to build more often than I break as I move through this world.

And every year I return to that place and I add a few more rocks, so that now my father the mountain stands still taller than before; so that now as ever I stand before you, ever in his shadow.

Pushing Up The Daisies

Flowers grow in the spots where you've buried him.

Little white flowers growing in thick sprays of light, brightening up the lawn. It's peculiar how fertile he apparently is.

It's a fun experiment, and you should be able to keep him alive for at least a couple more weeks, so you keep testing it.

There's plenty of him left for a few more bits of the garden.

You've got him pushed up close to the window so he can see the fruits of your labour.

It's hard to say how he feels about it, though.

You buried his tongue first.

The Ladykiller

"Just up here, Detective Inspector." the young officer said as he led her through to the body.

"Hmm… certainly looks familiar. The signature?"

"A flower, ma'am. Just like the other four."

"And our hold-back? Is this our lady, or another copy-cat?"

"Looks like the same uneven join on the final petal, ma'am." He smiled to himself. "I never thought I'd end up learning so much about knitting."

"It's crochet, Feathers. Not knitting. I suppose you still have a bit to learn on the subject, then?" He blushed bright and looked away. She leaned closer to the body, counting wounds. She stopped at ten. The killer was either getting more angry, or less controlled.

She raised her head to properly take in their surroundings. A secluded, shaded space, as with the other victims. A dark and foreboding alleyway.

"So. What was this ready looking gentleman doing down here do we suppose, Feathers?"

"Well, he's known, ma'am. He's a nasty one. We've had him on the hook for at least three home invasions that I can remember, but the victims always flinch from testifying. Always old ladies, ma'am. He terrifies them." He paused.

"Something more to say, Feathers?"

"Just… can't help thinking we're all a bit better off without him. And the other victims, as it turns out. Whoever this old dear is, however she's managing to get the better of them, difficult to think she's in the wrong. This seems like justice."

"You surprise me, Feathers." she tutted, and turned to look up at him, her expression severe. "Our job is to uphold the law, not to chase justice. Are you some kind of anarchist?"

"No, ma'am!" he exclaimed, admonished.

"Relax, Feathers. I'm playing with you." she said, facing the body again to hide her smile. "It is hard not to admire our perpetrator's pluck. But still, we have a job to do. Allowing our feelings to let us deviate too far from it is a treacherous road to go down."

"Yes, ma'am."

She looked around to see if there was anyone else in the immediate vicinity to hear them. There wasn't.

"Still, we *do* have a lot of other crimes to solve at the moment, don't we? Perhaps prioritising our workload is the order of the day, here."

She got up off her haunches, and turned toward him.

"I'll be back at the station." she said.

"Yes ma'am." he replied.

They exchanged a smile, and moved on.

Stranger Abroad

Boil it down to fundamentals. I am in here. They are out there. You can make the most complex situations digestible if you reduce them to the basics. Soon they will try and get inside. Soon they will try and come in here and get me.

It started with the old lady. Up in some village or other in Cyprus, in the mountains. Brown leather skin. Sitting on the doorstep, half not seeing with that one bad eye. Her lips curled back, her graveyard grin.

I wake up before I've even realised that I've fallen asleep. The whole place knows that I'm here by now. A crack in the wood of the barn door shows more of them out there than there were before. Mostly old folk and women now, but soon enough the men will come in from the fields, or somewhere else.

I lay my head back on my backpack.

Of course, I didn't put it together at the time, but it actually started six months before the mountain village, in a small hamlet in Thailand. That was where I first saw her.

The brown leather. That cemetery smile.

It just wasn't till Cyprus, so many places later, that I realised that I recognised those tombstone teeth. The peculiar feeling of familiarity that I'd felt in so many of these remote settlements coalesced, like the milky film in her fish-eye.

It was the same old lady!

The knowledge chased at my heels as I fled the country.

The sound of the door rattling in the frame brings me round once again. Loud male voices bellow, rage infected. I am in the uncanny valley. The sounds they make are formed from familiar anatomy, which makes their incoherence to me all the more distressing. If there are words, they mean nothing to me, the language alien.

I had run from place to place, trying to get further away, further ahead. Every time she was there before me, saying nothing. Just staring through me, smiling.

Sometimes she'd cackle laughter at something an aged companion said. I began to form a clearer understanding of what was happening. The people with her were from the other places too. They never moved on me. They never got the chance. I always noticed them before they noticed me. I always ran.

Through the cracks, I watch the assembled, the whole village turned out to see what is going on. A younger man that I have seen everywhere else before stands apart, looks in my direction. Then he calls back into the mob, and I see something bobbing above them, toward us. The hard and familiar shape of a shotgun.

I look at the other shotgun, the one in here with me, discarded in the corner. I already know that it is empty.

By the time I arrived in this place, months had passed since Cyprus. Exhausted, harried, and she was here, too. Walking past me on the street like I was nobody, like what they were doing to me didn't mean a damn thing to her.

Horror had somehow evolved into anger. I didn't even understand that I wasn't scared any more until I already had the old woman's wrists in my hands. I screamed my questions at her, although truth be told I don't know exactly what I asked. My words were all spit and fury. After so long running I think I may have forgotten how to make myself understood.

And I couldn't understand what she was screaming back, so I leaned in closer, feeling the bones of her wrists grind into dust against each other.

Because I leaned in, the butt of the shotgun failed to connect with the back of my head.

Her weapon-swinging friend was an old man with the same tanned leather skin. I recognised him, of course.

He was weak, and I took the gun from him easily. The last few months had made me spry. A hand hard in the centre of his chest put him on his backside in the road, looking lost. Without thinking I slammed the wooden stock of the shotgun into the bridge of his nose, and he fell onto his back, slack.

The woman wouldn't stop crying, wouldn't answer my questions.

I had expected her skin to feel rough under my fingertips, but it broke like parchment.

The shotgun outside is now in the hands of the young man. He heads for the door between us. I look over at the old man's shotgun, now empty, and I have no doubt that the blast from the one outside can get through this door that I have tried to brace shut.

Before today, I had never fired or even held a gun. Never used force on another human. I was shocked to discover that it was very easy.

You know, it really all started before Cyprus. Before Thailand, even. I remember this now that things have become so simple.

I'm not sure now whether keeping my job and Rachel got so hard because I couldn't cope with the city any more, or if it was the other way around. But once I lost both, once I had nothing left, I had no choice but to get out.

I got what money I had left out of my account. The cashier looked at me the same way Rachel had that morning, the same mix of pity and disgust. For that brief moment it was as if they were the same person.

I bought a backpack and a tube ticket to Gatwick, and that was that. The city, all of the cities, were just too confusing to me, just too many different faces, all the same. I had to get away.

I think I'm going to open the door before the man outside blows it to splinters. I feel calmer now. I feel sure that I can make them understand. They are all so familiar to me. We should be able to talk the same language, where I am now.

Where *am* I, anyway? Canada? New Zealand?

When I left the old lady on her doorstep, I no longer recognised her.

A Tough Room

So, this is where he works, the big man with the straight razor. See him moving slowly cross the room; you wouldn't have thought they made them that big, and you sure as fuck wouldn't have imagined a guy that vast would be so slick and delicate with his blade.

This guy; we've never been able to track down where this guy takes them to do his work. My organisation, the people I work for, they maybe don't want to know the fine details for the sake of plausible deniability, but they at least like to have a sense of things, have some clue of where the bodies are buried. But this guy, despite his considerable bulk; we've never been able to catch him when he picks a… a 'package' up. And we've never been able to find this place.

Who knows, maybe the guy has more than one safe place to take them. Sure as fuck, none of the dumb bastards I've sent to follow him have ever seen one of them. Well, the ones that came back haven't, anyway. Professional courtesy says that we never ask him about the soldiers that vanish without a trace in his wake.

The Demon Barber - as he's known to wise-guys like me that're in the know - he only gets used for special jobs. You need to send a message to some motherfucking prick who doesn't know to do his dealing off your territory, you just throw a few bills to a cornerboy with a glint in his eye; he'll cap that wannabe gangsta in broad daylight and the job is dusted and done. But you need an attorney extinct, or a federal witness to enter your own private relocation program? You cut a deal with the Barber.

In fact, I'm the guy who brokers that deal; at least for my organisation. I don't know much more about the guy than anyone else, but I'm the Caprelli family fixer in this burg, and that means that you want something like that done, you go through me. There are about a half dozen guys we use for messy jobs, and the Barber is one of them. And as far as I knew, I was the only one in my crew who had a hotline to the motherfucker.

So, how'd I end up here, if I don't know where *here* is?

Fuck if I know, is my answer to that question. Someone high up obviously heard something about me that they didn't like, or hell, maybe even cousin Joe found out that I was banging his bangle-wearing bitch of a wife alternate Thursdays, I don't know.

All I do know is I pass out in front of the tube watching old cop shows, then come awake with cold feet, zip-tied to that old barber's chair over there, and all I can see are white tiles and my clothes in a pile over in the corner. After a few minutes of working out that my mouth isn't working, like I've just been to the dentist or some shit, I notice a shadow crossing my face, and roll my eyes in that direction. While I'm processing the giant egg-shape of this guy, a meaty hand grabs my hair from the other side, and forces my head down over the shampoo basin that I haven't noticed before.

I don't get to feel the razor as it slides across my Adam's apple, because by the time the shock subsides I'm already out of myself, over here on the other side of the room, watching it all happen.

All I can think while I watch him holding me over the basin, cold water running, is that when there's that much blood it doesn't look real *at all*. All those times watching slasher flicks and bitching about the fake blood? I won't be doing that again. Well, course, *obviously* I won't be, but you know what I mean, right?

And so, I'm standing here, watching the big guy as he quietly goes about slicing me up, breaking me down into easily disposable pieces, and I'm feeling pretty detached. Kinda like I should be angry or upset but it's like I'm on heroin and everything is real far away. The Demon Barber is grunting softly as he works on some particularly strong muscle tissue, and I'm actually laughing, thinking *well yes, ma'am, I do work out… how could you tell?* The laughing and the grunting, though, I barely hear them… they echo like I'm underwater.

As he's finishing off his clean-up I start to wonder, *well, then, what's next? Come on, motherfucker, where's the bright light…? Where's the next place?* Which, you know, is wishful thinking on my part. That I might get to the good place. But I figure I'm entitled. It's not like I ever actually *capped* a son-of-a-bitch.

Nothing happens though, and he's finishing up, and then he's switching off the light. And when it's dark in here I look down at my hand, and I can kind of see it still, like it's a negative image of itself.

And there are other shapes hanging out there now, floating in the darkness of the room, like I'm a broad in a peepshow and all of the johns have stroked in a coin at the same time. They're all looking at me, flat and dull like they don't give a shit. And I'm on display with my titties out, so to fucking speak. When I call out to them, ask them "what the fuck?", they don't react and I'm underwater again.

Then I start to recognise faces and it's like my high school reunion, because it's all the losers that I ever dropped a line on to the Barber, all the snitches and the skimmers and the wise-guys and the jerks, and that's when I get it. This is it, now; this is in-between, where I get to float in the dark until the next time the guy with my old life gives the Demon Barber a job, and me and all the other guys he ever laid his blade on get to watch, again and again, in our own little peepshows in the dark.

Getting Out

The inside of the car smells like four blokes full of nerves and chemicals had been sitting in it for a bit too long.

In the passenger seat Ted stares out his window, eyes fixed on the exit point, tries to keep his fingers from tapping at his thighs. Ballard just keeps talking. *Fucking dreamers and amateurs, always talking*, Ted thinks.

"...And we're trying to sort ourselves out in this new office - basically a cupboard with desks - and we've got the air conditioning running like a fan, just trying to get the air moving in there. And so, he comes in, looks around, goes over to the air-con controls, and just changes the settings. Walks out."

Despite himself, Ted has to ask.

"Eh? So, what did you do?"

"Well, nothing. Not much I *could* do. He's a manager."

"This was your boss?"

"Not *my* manager. Just *a* manager. There are a lot of them at that place. Often go around in pairs. And… get this. He does it again, the next day."

"And, what? You just took it?"

"I mean," Ballard shrugs, "he's a manager."

Ted stares at Ballard for a second, a look that says that he's never heard anything so fucking stupid, and snorts, dismissing the driver.

They both stare out the window at the fire exit again.

"This is taking too long," says Ted.

Ballard sneaks a look at his watch.

"They've got a couple more minutes on the clock," he says. "Anyway, the shift change should give them about five minutes each way with the guards."

Ted gives him a surprised look.

"The guards here are lazy fuckers. I've watched them the last few nights, in between checking the route. This isn't my first job, you know."

Another thirty seconds pass slow. Ballard can't help it with the nervous energy again.

"What are you going to do with the money?" he asks.

"Are you my wife?" Ted snaps, then cools. "Ah, I don't know. We haven't had a decent holiday in two years, so maybe that. There's some stuff needs doing to our house. And I'm trying to save a bit, for the kids."

"Nice," says Ballard, only half listening. He's excited about his bit. "Nice. I'm going to use my share to get out. I promised myself… one good job, and I'm getting out."

"You only just got in!" Ted says. But he's starting to warm to the guy.

"No, I mean…" Ballard looks out the driver's side window, where there's nothing but a brick wall.

"Look, I wasn't always a civilian. My first job out of school was as a driver. Bits of cabbie work, bits of chauffeuring, and a lot of this." He waves around the inside of the car to indicate the job they're on. "I was fucking good, n'all. That's how I met Derek, and why he let me drive this job."

Ted is interested now, but only shows it as much as you're meant to.

"But after about five years, things started to get a bit too edgy. In the space of a year two of our bosses got taken down by the filth, and then a meeting with a new contact went messy - I got us out of there but Derek got cut up. I was too young and it all felt a bit unstable. I had a good head for systems, and enough money saved to do a few courses at college. Got myself an office job and got serious."

"Right," says Ted. "So, you went straight and got boring. And now you're on your mid-life crisis. Fuck me, our lives depend on a thrill-seeker." He laughs, sardonic.

"Nah, mate, it's not like that," Ballard says. Then, interrupted, nods at the fire exit as it slams open, their colleagues rushing through carrying over-full duffle bags. "Better help them in."

Ballard taps his fingers in a rhythm against the steering wheel, ready, his eyes on the open exit looking out for security. Ted accounts for the team; Derek in behind Ballard, Ennis next to him, Ted back in place.

"Go," signals Ted, firm but steady. "Masks off." he reminds Derek and Ennis.

Without a word Ballard drives, firm but steady. Quickly out of the alleyway, within the speed limit on the road, taking a left then two rights to drive calmly past the front of the place they'd just robbed, now alive with activity. Sirens in the distance, and then police arriving around them, and Ballard keeping it together the whole time. Ted is impressed; he gets a sense that the driver would keep it just as cool if they were being actively pursued.

"Half the trick is making sure nobody chases you in the first place," Ballard says to him, reading his look. A surge of relief starts Derek and Ennis laughing in the back seat.

Later, after the safe house, the two of them alone in the car again, on the way to get rid of it.

"I've never been into thrills," Ballard says. He's clearly kept the earlier conversation in his head.

"That's not me at all."

"Innit?" Ted says.

"It's the chaos, the lack of sense. I can manage short bursts of it, like today on a job, but I can't handle it constantly. I quit the life because outside of the work, everything seemed fucked. For a bit there we didn't know who to trust, and it felt like a normal life would be safer."

"Yeah." Ted is thinking about his younger brother, who did well at school and went to Uni and got a nice job and has a nice house and two holidays a year, one abroad. "I can see that."

"Thing is, work like *this*; I have one boss, and maybe he reports to someone, and they report to someone, but I have one boss. And the way it works, I drive well, I do a good job, I don't screw anybody over, nine years out of ten this life looks after me if I look after it." Ballard glares at his knuckles as he drives. "The rules tend to stay roughly the same. No reshuffles or policy meetings or committees or whatever. And the stakes are too high for power-plays that don't make any fucking sense."

"I can see that, too," Ted says, and this time he's thinking about what he'd have done to the guy who kept messing with the air if he'd been in Ballard's place, the story he told earlier. Messing with the fucking air, though.

"So, yeah. I'm going to use my share to get myself clear; hand in my resignation and try to earn an honest living thieving."

Ted starts laughing at that, and eventually Ballard joins in.

My Best Friend

My best friend is a rock.

There are people who scoff at that. People who tell me "that is just a rock".

To those people I say "fuck you". To those people I say "My friend is not 'just' a rock. My friend is strong, and smooth, and reliant. And if you cracked my friend open, you would see that inside my friend is crystalline, and delicate, and beautiful. But you would never see that, because you could never crack her open. She is too strong. She would crack you open first.

To those people I say "If I cracked you open, what would I see? Filth and gristle and meat."

To those people I say "You are nothing compared to my friend."

And I lift my friend in front of their eyes, and test my friend's weight in a meaningful way.

Usually, those people say very little to me after that.

One Of Us

There's a bottle of unbranded vodka on the table, and nothing much else.

Nothing much else in here at all, in fact. The room is another nameless motel room, in another faceless motel. Paid for in cash from a bundle left for me by the client at a safety deposit box at the station. When I'm in town to work I tend not to use one of the safe-houses, unless events conspire against me.

I look at the bottle, run a fingertip along the ridged curve of the screw-top.

I don't like vodka. Vodka is Ivan's drink.

I don't like explosions, either; loud noises play hell with my constitution. Ivan is the demolitions expert.

The cap makes a cracking noise as I open the bottle for the first time. I take an exploratory sniff. Even the odour – something people will swear vodka doesn't have, but I can definitely smell it – sets something off. Ivan's voice, in my ear, close by.

For years, I didn't know that the alters even existed. When you're in the care system most adults barely notice you at all, so it's not surprising nobody noticed that I'd black out for days at a time, and someone else would take over.

It took the rigid structure of a stretch in juvie for the cracks to really show; there was nothing *but* scrutiny inside, and when one of the others – Spinning Jenny I think – assaulted one of the other inmates, I was sent to see a shrink. Within six months she and I had established the fact of my condition, and had even sketched out a vague roster of the other personas.

You're supposed to call it DID, now… Dissociative Identity Disorder is what you're supposed to call it. For some reason Multiple Personality Disorder wasn't considered appropriate any more. The new name sounds more like an illness, but the older term carried a sort of inner truth to it.

They *are* personalities; as much as any personality is. Whether a person's character is a cluster of chemical triggers, a bundle of choices and memories accumulating to make patterns of behaviour, or something else altogether; whatever it is, it applies to the alters as much as to anyone else.

I'm not aware of what's going on when one of the others is in the driving seat, but they know about each other; communicate with each other, even, or at least seem to. After a while they even started to get in touch with me, either through shrinks or messages left in notepads, on mirrors and, in one particularly visceral show of petulance, in feces on a wall. We've reached a kind of consensus over time.

I need Ivan for the job I've got on tonight. He speaks close in my ear as he seeps in, and reminds me about the gun. I take it out of the paper bag on the floor at my feet and put it on the table next to the vodka.

This is the nearest I get to being aware of the others, during the transition from me to them. I didn't used to feel anything, but as we've started working together more, I've started to recognise their character traits as they come on in.

None of this would have been possible without the help of the best of the shrinks. He was also the last of them. I suspect that what I do for money now wasn't what he had in mind. Together we'd managed to identify thirteen alters. We were even talking assimilation by then, which obviously at least one of the personalities didn't like. I'm guessing Anodyne Annie. She's always been the persona most likely to sabotage the whole, and also the only one who doesn't like to announce her arrival. None of the others get off on pretending to be me.

Whoever it was, they did a number on us. Over a few sessions, she seduced the good doctor. And then she dropped the youngest of the alters into the driving seat, midway through a tryst.

The youngest of the alters is me at six years old. Of course, she isn't really; *I* was me at six years old. But we were practically the same person back then, and she stayed frozen in place. She still uses the same name, if you can believe that.

She suffers from DID too, if you can believe *that*. It was being thrown into the lap of the doctor that did it, I think. We've never been able to work out the extent of her condition. She doesn't come out that often any more.

For a few weeks afterward, I didn't really know what was going on. I was in and out of consciousness and as far as I could tell I was living on the street for a while there. When I finally got it back together, I discovered that I was on the run. Ivan had visited the good doctor one night, and left his body in pieces for his staff to find.

The alters, it turns out, had developed some particularly useful skills over time. Nothing that could get us by in the overground working world but, like Ivan, each had picked up tricks that serve us well in a particular line of work.

From Lazy Susan, who can work the hardest grift without breaking a sweat, to Spinning Jenny's knack with knives, together there aren't many contract jobs we can't pull off.

Me? My only real skill is holding it all together.

I take a swig of vodka and invite Ivan all the way in. Tonight, something bad is going to happen, somewhere outside this hotel room.

I'm glad I won't be there to see it.

Near Roger's Point

It's bitter cold and I know it; I shouldn't be out here on foot by myself. But there are some experiences worth a bit of suffering for, and history tells me this is one of them. My breath plumes out of my parka and mists the air around me as I go.

The world is so vast and empty here, and you can see so far that I feel the curve of the earth under me. The wind and cold and distance I've walked add to that feeling, of a gentle but persistent slope. Pulling my feet through the damned snow adds to the relentlessness.

It's only a matter of hiking around five miles from the nearest track, but you don't want to get caught out here in a whiteout, and that is a fact that you can take to the bank.

But then I'm there, and the sight near takes my breath away.

You might have heard about the incident down at McCormick Cross a while back, or at least heard one of the many stories about it. The news reported it as any number of different things and finally seemed to settle on a consensus of "natural ecological disaster". Fifty miles north, we at Roger's Point knew the truth of it…

See, as the closest neighbours we were the first place that the survivors thought to come, some of them in vehicles, some on sleds. Some sad few, what needed immediate medical assistance on arrival made the trek on foot, and only God knew how they did it.

Although of course when you see this here vista you understand *exactly* how they did it. Because you'd drag yourself on your belly across broken glass to get away from the glorious horror that I see in front of me.

Froze in place, some of them missing parts, most of them upright but some crawling down on all fours; all of them human but not quite. A frosting of ice across their skins, they look like storm damaged trees. And even after all these years, you can hear them moaning deep in their throats, and the slightest creaking shifts of their joints keep you edgy and alert.

Hundreds of them spread out even, all stopped dead (and if *that* ain't a turn of phrase and a half) on their way after the leftovers of McCormick Cross. If you stand too close to them, they can fill your vision, and the dim-heard groans can drive you part-crazy.

We never did know how they all of them knew to follow the survivors, whether it was sound or smell or something else, or if they just sensed folk out there in the cold and dark in Roger's Point.

And none really believed the hysterical tales that our neighbours brought to us till they came out looking and found… this. Even then, realisation takes a slim while to set in. These things look like people. And then you notice how they're upright even with parts of their heads or bodies missing that shouldn't be.

It gets colder by increments the further north you get up here, and away from the towns it gets worse again, so we figured that things with no heat in them to begin with wouldn't be able to get as far as them that had some warmth in their bones and the sense to keep themselves protected, and that must be what had happened here. We also figured, rightly or wrongly, that telling the truth of it wouldn't be worth the worry; either it would be written off as more backwoods Alaskan nonsense, or it would attract all the wrong kind of attention.

So, we keep our counsel, and we keep away from this dangerous forest of the undead.

Except every now and then I make the trip out here, to stand in awe at the weirdness and monstrosity in the world. I know it's a bad idea. But I keep a safe distance from the frozen, outstretched hands, and I never let my guard down.

I don't know, I guess I find this place strangely comforting. My mother was a McCormick Cross survivor; one of the walkers. She and my daddy

met when he was giving medical aid to the refugees as they came in. Theirs was a romance born out of this horror that surrounds me. Now that they are both gone, I look for ways to feel close to their memory, and this place and these abominations have proved the greatest way I've found.

I always find that it is best to leave as the euphoric reminder of my parent's love hits its peak, and before terror or maudlin feelings start to kick in. I tip the hood of my parka to the nearest of the zombies, and turn to make the long trek home.

A Persistent Yield

When I was very small, we moved into a very small house on a very quiet street. My parents, my siblings, and I.

There was a very small garden. More like a large patio, with a tiny square of dirt at one end. I would later learn that it was the first garden that my father could call his own.

He had always wanted to grow food, so he planted food. In that first year he tried to grow very little, and the garden yielded less. By the end of the summer less than half a dozen courgettes, twenty cherry tomatoes, and a handful of runner beans were all that made it from the garden into my mother's tiny kitchen.

It is normal for adults to pass on wisdom to their offspring. Often that knowledge is aspirational.

My father had a theory about human potential that he shared with me many times through my childhood. These conversations were less inspiring than I have been led to believe such conversations are supposed to be.

My father's theory about human potential was this:

Exploring one's potential is an exercise that should be undertaken with the utmost caution and absolutely no expectation, because potential is not the infinite resource of legend, and in some folk there is a lot less of it than in others.

My father was successful in his business, and my mother was successful in her way, and we moved from that very small house into a less small one. And later on, we moved again, and again, and when it was finally time for me to leave the family home, the family home was quite large, in expansive grounds, in an expensive village.

My father continued to grow food in one corner of the garden, whichever house that garden happened to be attached to, and over the years more and more space was given over to those rows of dirt. But every year, without variance, the same harvest made its way to the kitchen and the dinner table. Less than half a dozen courgettes, twenty cherry tomatoes, and a handful of runner beans.

In the years where he tried to grow something else, either alongside those three crops or in place of them, the different crop failed completely.

Still my father persisted, year after year. Because, he said, he enjoyed the process.

I have never really decided whether or not I agree with my father's theory. I found my father - and to a lesser extent my mother - complicated and difficult to fathom, and this is not something that has changed since having my own house, and my own garden, and my own family.

But for one thing. As conventional wisdom understands it, the parental capacity for love - like individual human potential - is not a finite affair. But from personal experience I believe that my mother and my father had enough love for almost exactly two point four children. I believe this as a certainty, and I am the youngest of three siblings.

As I type this my wife is heavy with our third child. I cannot help but wonder what my own potential for love is.

Conventional

It's a little after lunchtime on the first day of the show, and the malaise of the small fry among big fish has long taken hold.

"Alright, mate. I got you a coffee." Dave said to his companion behind the table.

"Alright." replied James from his perch.

"Looks busy." Dave looked around, trying to find a way back to his seat next to his friend. "Ah, balls." he said, resigned. Placing the two coffees on their long table, he hunkered down, lifted back the sheet that settled like a skirt along the table's length, and scooted underneath. A few seconds later he bobbed up awkwardly alongside James, and settled into his seat with a sigh.

The two old friends sipped their coffee in silence for a few minutes, watching the crowds passing their spot.

"What are this lot up to?" Dave asked.

"Queueing for Thor." James replied.

"Hmph."

"I know. Not even worth bothering unless you're one of the big guns, is it?"

"Ah, it's not so bad. At least we get to look at all the beautiful people."

"They're pretty, but they're incredibly young. And they only ever dress as someone famous, or famous-ish. Never anyone we have anything to do with."

"True enough."

And with that they fell silent, drinking their coffee and waiting out the end of the first day of the convention, when they could get to the serious drinking with their fellow gods, the tiny and the gigantic. Dave, the God of Successful One Night Stands, and James, the God of Men Called James.

The Task At Hand

Surveying the scene, I wonder:

Is there anything more evocative than the sight of a child's toys, neatly arranged, and sprayed erratically with blood?

I consider this for a few more moments, then set to the task at hand.

Driving Baby Home

The city has been decked out for the holidays with a total lack of restraint. The streetlights, the decorations, the headlights of other cars, reflections off windows and the slick roads. Giving me a killer headache, what my dad calls a "bastard behind the eyes". At a stoplight, I press my eyelids down, push the knuckles of my fingers down into them to try and give some relief. The bright spots still intrude through the soft skin, white shapes swimming in the red, like something pure, drowned and drifting in blood.

When I open them again the light has changed, and the car and I sit idle at a crossroads, the only vehicle left on the road. I push down on the gas and we both lurch on. I try not to think about the things behind me; the thing in the trunk, and the mess I left back at the apartment. After things went bad with Jenny.

A half-hour later and I'm almost out, almost on the open highway. Not even been driving for an hour yet and I'm already losing it. A song keeps cycling through my head and I can't shake it. I don't know the tune that well, just the one line, and it just repeats, over and over.

Driving home for Christmas.

Fucked if I know what I'm going to say to mom and dad. Haven't seen them in four years; they haven't heard from me in nearly as many months. I have no idea why running to them occurred to me. I dread seeing them at the best of times.

Less than an hour down, upward of four hours left on the road, and I'm already drifting, panicking. I guess that that's why I stop for the guy.

I don't spot him straight away so I have to swerve in and slam on the brakes, and he has to jog a little to catch up to me. His piece of cardboard tells me that he's heading to the same place as I am. When he opens the passenger door and pokes his head in, I see that he's around eighteen, twenty. Gives me around ten years on him. I fight down the urge to tell him that he's heading in the wrong direction.

"Buddy", he tells me, when asked his name. He seems a little nervous, holds his backpack on his lap. Good looking kid, dark hair long enough that he has to keep shaking his head, flick it out of his face. He doesn't look like a Buddy but what the hell, I'm not a cop, I just need some company to keep my head straight for the long drive.

We're driving around an hour, making good time out of the city, making a little small talk. I don't find out much about him but then I'm not asking. Neither is he. After all this time he starts to relax a little, decides the bag is getting heavy, tries to fit it into the foot-space in front of him. It isn't a big car and he struggles. When I glance over to see what he's doing he's bending forward, and I notice the hard metal bulge of the gun sticking out the back of his waistband like something out of a movie.

He notices me noticing and nerves flicker across his face again, like he's trying to work out whether to try and look dangerous or go the other way, but I get the feeling his nature would get the better of him if he tried to push either stance too far.

I shrug, and look out the window, my message of 'what the fuck do I care?' pretty clear.

He struggles some more with the bag, and I take pity on him.

"Hold on." I say, and pull the car to the side of the dead highway.

I pop the trunk, and when he looks back in the direction of the sound, I nod and say "Go ahead."

"Thanks," he says, and gets out.

A few moments later I hear him yelp, and yell, "What the fuck is that?"

Damn. I did too good a job of pushing it to the back of my mind. I get out, go round, and see him standing a few yards away from the back of the car, staring. I follow his look down into the trunk. I'm guessing it isn't the other assorted clutter he's freaking about. I'm guessing that it's the large sample jar, green tinted in the moonlight. It's big enough to fit a human head. The shape swimming in the turbulent mess of formaldehyde in there is barely visible, but unmistakable all the same. The brain tries to retreat away from it, pretend it hasn't noticed the tiny fingers, the curve of the tiny head, and the result is more distressing, as if the object is less tangible, less real.

I cover the slippery curve of the jar with the grey blanket that I keep back there for emergencies. Hiding it calms him down some; enough at least to let me take the backpack and cram it down into the remaining space in the trunk. Slamming down the hood seems to snap him all the way back to the here and now. He looks at me quizzically.

"Inside." I say, "It's fucking cold out here."

Back in the car. It doesn't start first time, takes a little foreplay, a little coaxing. He stays quiet while I tease the rental to life. Once we're back underway I figure I might as well broach the subject so that he doesn't have to.

"The thing in the trunk," I say, "is my son."

"Your son?" he asks.

"Yeah." I say, look over at him, look back out onto the blacktop. "I'm taking him home to my parents' place. While I work things out."

"Right." he says. Looks at his hands. Then says "Right" again, but this time it's obvious that that's an end to it. He sighs, and the seat creaks gently as the tension seeps out of him for the first time, bleeding out into the car.

"You okay? You looked pretty freaked out."

"No. I mean, yeah. I'm just… it's been a hell of a day." he says, and grins.

"You want a drink?" I say, eyes off the highway again.

"Hell yeah." he replies, and I signal toward the glove-box, where the liquor is.

We share a drink, a few laughs, and drive on into the night, towards my home town, my parents, and whatever the fuck the future might bring.

What I Know Now

I hear a voice over the baby monitor. A voice from our baby son Luka's room, next door.

John doesn't stir. Of course, he doesn't. I turn and look at the back of his head, half convinced that he isn't asleep, that he's deliberately pretending he hasn't heard, but it's no good. I've been told by so many people that a mother has an uncanny ear for the sounds of their child in need that the notion has stuck, and I can't help but feel a tiny stab of pride that I'm better at this than he is. I try to tune in to the sounds from the little speaker, make out what they really are.

Every few weeks it'll sound like an actual-to-goodness human voice over the monitor. Not the sounds of a six-month-old baby but a full-grown person, making full-formed words. The first time we heard it, it horrified us. Luckily, we were visiting with my sister at the time, and she said "Nah, that happens with all the monitors… it's interference or room noises or something, not real voices", and that and a bit of a longer listen set us straight.

Now when it happens John gets fascinated with what he calls "pattern recognition"; how we can

217

pull together varied sounds and make them sound like voices in our heads, like people do with crying geese or such.

It still creeps me out a little, personally.

And there it is again. It might be a voice, or it might not. Which means it might be the sound of a strange man in Luka's nursery, or it might just be Luka waking in the night and trying out a new sort of cry to get our attention.

It has always struck me as strange when this happens that the parental instinct to protect one's young doesn't instantly kick in. Logically, why wouldn't I run in there as fast as I can just in case? Or wake John up so he can?

But I don't. And that earlier stab of pride becomes a tiny prick of guilt at what I identify in myself as fear and self-preservation if there's an intruder, or fear of embarrassment if there isn't.

I lie in the dark listening and try and work out what to do. I decide to shift noisily in my bed, see if that achieves anything.

The noises in the next room stop. At which point I realise that that doesn't actually prove anything. Maybe there's an intruder listening out for sounds of stirring from us, or maybe I'm just imagining the sounds. Useless.

I have to get up and see if the baby needs anything. That's the normal thing to do when you think they might need you in the night. No husband required.

There's someone standing over the cot bed. A little taller than me, and standing like a man. Yelling or running from the room to get my husband doesn't occur to me in my panic. I'm scared of what he might do to Luka if I stop watching him.

"Get out of here." I say, trying to keep my voice as neutral as possible, not wanting to startle him or show him my fear.

He turns toward me and now I can see past him to where Luka is lying awake in bed, smiling up at the stranger. My son catches sight of me and beams even wider. I look from him to the intruder, who is staring at me, a broad smile on his own face.

He looks familiar, but not enough that it calms me.

"I said get out!" I repeat, dimly aware that I'm in the way of his only exit.

"I'll only be a minute." he says. There's a weird expression on his face now.

He's got a nice face, actually. Pleasant without being *too* handsome. He actually looks a bit like John, though older. Much older maybe, but sometimes maybe not. There's something about that smile.

I reflexively look at Luka. He has stopped smiling at me and is now curled up, trying to find his feet in his sleeping bag.

I don't realise I'm still watching him until the man speaks again, startling me.

"I haven't been careful enough, I'm sorry. You shouldn't have heard me." He keeps smiling, but his eyes soften suddenly. "God, it's so good to see you again. I wasn't supposed to, but I'm glad. I haven't seen you in such a long time."

"What?" I blurt. "Who the hell *are* you? Why are you here?"

He keeps looking at Luka, who coos up at him, blows raspberries.

"We get to come back, you see, to share a few secrets. At the end… after the end, really, we get a few precious chances to visit here at the start."

He turns back to me.

"Don't worry mum… he won't really remember."

The three of us there, in the dark, me not really understanding what he just said, and I realise that I'm crying, and can't stop.

The Ghost Of Flight 721

Nobody fears the ghost of flight 721. It passes overhead, far above, where it cannot be seen except for the ethereal shades of the contrails it leaves behind it.

It haunts the terminal at Heathrow; the expectant travellers hear its name rattling through the Arrivals board as they stand and shiver against an unseasonably cold draught. It is in the spectral hiss and slither of a luggage belt always missing that one cargo bay's load. Flight 721 from Malaga, due in at around quarter past two, local time, six months previous. Departed, but never arrived.

The families of flight 721's crew and passengers occasionally look to the sky, hands shielding their eyes from the sun, blinking. They still receive the shadows of text messages, furtively clicked out to them from somewhere *up there*, where the polite but firm request to ensure all mobile phones are switched off still stands eternal. "*Been held up*," the messages say. "*Should b back in the next couple of hours.*" or "*I'm afraid I'm going 2 miss dinner.*"

They look to the sky, and then they scratch their foreheads absently, tut to themselves, and go about their business. It can't be helped, they think helplessly.

The Arrivals board rattles and clicks through again, the information constantly adjusting, the "Delay" statement for the 721 from Malaga dumbly rising up and on through higher increments. When it still only read 20 minutes there were people reading it. But the last person left after two days. He was waiting for his girlfriend to come back after a family holiday. He was planning to propose right there, on his knees in front of everyone. Now he waits for her at home. He figures just having stuck around this long for her will be quite romantic enough.

Nobody waits in the arrivals lounge for flight 721 anymore. The Arrivals board keeps updating, but no one is looking.

There has been no search for the remains of the plane. No headlines or grave announcements by a spokesman for the airline. These things have not happened, because the flight still continues.

It started out well enough. In fact, 'brakes off' occurred around five minutes early in Malaga with all passengers on board and settled. It crossed borders, land and sea without incident.

It was on approach to London that the first problem occurred. The pilot was asked to go around again, to allow an earlier delayed flight to land before him. This wasn't unusual so he acceded. Then there was a problem with his angle of approach, so he was told to abort and try again. By this point, weather conditions were deteriorating, and… Well, you see how these things can snowball.

The flight was only ever delayed for a few minutes at a time, so nobody really noticed the point when they stopped noticing it. Regular status reports come through from the crew, but they stopped being noted some time ago. The radio squawks these phantom messages into the control room to be ignored; they might as well be static or white noise. Ghosts in the machine.

Flight 721 had nothing wrong with it. The journey was and continues to be utterly routine, and as such has slipped away from the conscious world that by necessity has to concern itself with the things that go wrong, rather than those that continue to function within the acceptable margin for delays.

Apparently, ghost planes never need to refuel.

So, flight 721 still circles the airport, up there somewhere. Its passengers late, but not deceased.

The Road May Rise To Meet You, But The World Will Roll Against You

We're pacing through the half-arsed dark, and though he keeps lagging behind it's obvious who has the sprightlier step. Which is impressive, considering the state he was in the last time I saw him.

"Streets are quiet, aren't they?" he says, and it's not that odd an observation to make. On any normal day, sure, the only people awake would be farmers, posties and milkmen, just getting round to their breakfast. But this wasn't a normal day. When he'd turned up in my kitchen an hour earlier the sounds of screams and outrage and delight were echoing through the night, from every house within earshot, resonating through the peculiar mist that still stuck to the ground at our feet.

Now, though, there are no signs of life. Whatever life means. Not as far as we can tell. Not over the roaring in our ears and the sound of our bodies moving as we stride with purpose.

I don't want to stop moving. I know that if I do, and I leave a few moments for the blood to stop burring in my ears, I'll probably be able to hear activity within the houses. The sound of emotional chatter. The noise of impossible reunion.

Or else the blood won't stop rushing and the chaotic roar will take me all the way to where I'm obviously already heading, to the loony bin.

I tell him to keep it down and keep walking.

"Where are we going, anyway?" he asks half-heartedly. The haunted streets hold a fascination for him and he's full of energy, trying to take it all in, a sheen of eager sweat on his forehead.

I had hustled Ray out of the house as quickly as I could, before I'd even registered the oddness of him being there. Instinct had told me to get him away from Tanya and the baby, though I didn't believe he'd hurt them. I think I just knew that if we woke her up, and she came downstairs, I'd have to explain Ray's presence to her, and I didn't want to admit that I couldn't do that, or why.

Not that there was much fear of Tanya waking up. Since Jude's birth a couple of months ago she's usually exhausted by ten, asleep on the couch, and once I rouse her from there and drag her up to bed, she'll be spark out till seven or eight the next morning.

My sleep patterns are considerably more disrupted. Jude has, quite miraculously, been sleeping through most of the night almost since we got her home, but with night feeds and the rest I'm still not quite straight with the extra body in the house. I wake up at regular intervals and have to go in and check on her.

I was lying awake, fruitlessly trying to grab a couple more hours before the alarm, when the sounds started up in the world outside our window. People squealing, and squawking, and yelling. I guessed that a house party had kicked out somewhere, and briefly checking that Tanya was still asleep, I rolled out of bed and went to get myself a snack.

Ray had been sitting at the kitchen table, still enough that I didn't register him properly till I recognised him. I forgot all about food. I also found I'd forgotten – or perhaps my life experience had failed to train me in the first place – how to deal with finding someone you haven't seen in nearly thirty years in your kitchen at four in the morning.

After a few exclamations and choice words exchanged, I decided we were going for a walk. I left him on his own in there for a matter of moments while I as quickly and quietly as possible found myself some clothes, and bustled him out.

"You not going to talk to me, then?" he asks after a few more minutes of silence.

"In a minute." I reply, the words forming in puffs in the cold, misting air. I'm feeling cold everywhere except on my cheeks, which are flushed red, but that film of sweat seems to cover him now, forming in patches through his clothes. "I need to think."

"Jesus, okay. Sorry I asked." he says, thrusting his hands in his pockets, out-pacing me in a moment. "Do you at least have your Walkman on you?"

I check my pockets and find my phone which I hand to him, untangling the earphones without breaking pace.

He holds it, examining it as we walk. He turns to me.

"What's *this*?" he says.

"Oh, sorry." I say, and take it back for a second. "Hang on. I've got a playlist that'll be… Hm. I've been putting together for Jude."

"Playlist?" he asks, but he knows what to do with the earphones as I sort the app out for him. I plug him in and hand the phone back. When the music starts, he nods his head in appreciation.

"…Nice!" he says.

"Yeah. It's so she'll know what her dad listened to growing up. Right now, that's the nineties you're listening to."

"Oh, right." he plays with the touchscreen, and works it out pretty quick.

We walk in silence again.

He bobs his head until he hits a track he doesn't recognise.

"Who's this?" he says, showing me the display. It's from later in the decade, Britpop, female-fronted.

"Oh, yeah… they're alright. Not together any more, though. She was a bit hot."

"It's alright."

"Yeah." I say, and it's starting to sink in properly. It's Ray.

Some of the music is a revelation. He doesn't know what the fuck is going on with modern hip-hop, but he's almost certain he's heard some of the British stuff before, until I tell him he can't have. There's some transgressive stuff from the early oughts that makes him laugh, and some jangly and discordant bands Tanya and I just started listening to that confuse him for a second, but he keeps going back and listening to them again.

It's weird. There's a misting of liquid where his skin is visible, a halo around his face and his hands. Millions of little droplets of water, vibrating in the air.

I walk in silence next to him, the tiny trebly hiss of music coming from the tiny buds in his ears telling me which song he's hearing.

We get to where we're going well before dawn. I hesitate at the gate.

"Ha!" he says, coiling the earphone lead around his hand. He hands the phone and the lead back to me. "I thought we might be coming here."

It takes a few minutes to find what I'm looking for. The lampposts lining the lanes have been left on all night every night since a spate of quite nasty assaults took place here a couple of years ago, but it's still quite hard to read the inscriptions on the stones. It's been a couple dozen years since either of us has been here, anyway, so we're not sure where to look.

But eventually I *do* find the grave, and we both stand over it. For a few moments we're silent.

And then:

"Hm. This is a bit weird."

"Yeah." I say.

"I've never actually seen this, you know?"

"No?" I ask, genuinely curious.

"Mm. Had other things on my mind, and it seemed a bit… morbid, you know?"

"I suppose so." I say, but I've formed a few questions, now, and I feel the need to ask them. I can't decide which one to start with, so I ask the one that seems to get to the crux of a few of them at once. "Ray, what the fuck is going on?"

He ponders for a second before answering.

"Well, I don't know, really. There were quite a few years of not a lot going on. Just lots of nothing much. A lot of people in a room, talking nowt. And then suddenly I'm here, all pulled together and buzzing around."

"But… you're dead, dude."

"Well, yeah." He rubs his arm nervously, a mannerism I remember. His arm seems to fall apart wetly under his fingernails, but when he stops it bubbles for a second, and then it's as if nothing had happened again.

"So, why visit me? I haven't…" I bite back my first pass at that sentence, and say "…seen you in forever, and don't your family still live in town? Didn't you want to visit them?"

I hadn't thought about Ray since a few months after he died. He had been part of a large extended social group that I stumbled into when I was studying. I was a transplant to the town, here for the University, but most of them were natives and had known each other for years.

The glue of that particular group had been music and drugs. Nothing too hard – indie pop, sample-heavy, and rave, happy and hyper – and the drugs were picked to match. I took a lot of acid with those guys.

Ray and I had similar neuroses, and similar senses of humour, and when the pack was tripping we'd find ourselves in sync pretty well. We'd get the same daft notions. One night, for example, Ray remembered that I was borrowing a proper camera from Uni, with a separate flash and everything, and we decided that we would sit in a dark room with my album covers and the camera and see if we could burn classic images onto our retinas.

Fond, stupid memories. But altogether I was probably only part of the group-proper for a couple of years before it started to dissipate. People got jobs, or went on their *own* way to study in other towns. You'd see them in pubs or clubs every now and then down through the years, and it'd be nice. But we'd moved on, because people do.

Ray had stayed local but I hadn't seen him for around three or four months before I heard that he had died. Some random accident. A guy driving his kids to school had got distracted somehow and slid his car off the road onto the verge. An incident that the occupants of the car probably would have forgotten all about in a couple of weeks, none of them injured. If they hadn't hit Ray. He was walking to work, country roads with no footpath, just the grass. His back to the traffic the way that you're supposed to.

It had been an incredibly sad piece of news for everybody to hear, but more: it was an imposition on the expected natural order of things. One expects for loved ones to get ill, get old, or die, and expects it to hurt, but people you just *know* –that you don't see for ages until you do– they become more like landmarks in your physical world than individuals. You don't know them that well any more but you know which bars they'll be propping up, or which shops you'll bump into them in. When *they* go, it's surreal. You suddenly miss them, even though you haven't up till then.

Loads of faces cycled back into the town from across the country for the funeral, and it was good to see them. But it also served as another reminder that as life went on, we would have less and less in common. Even back then, a few new partners and spouses were left at home, or people had to leave early to make it to important meetings at work the next day "back home".

Ray never got to leave that scene but the rest of us carried on. Found life coming at us in waves as sure as Brit Pop gave way to Shit Pop gave way to whatever came next, and the only person that stayed persistent in a person's life turned out to be themselves, aside from the rare people they managed to trap in close enough trajectories to their own.

Ray doesn't answer straight away. He looks up at the moon and then off to one side, out of the cemetery.

"Let's walk." he says, and starts off in the direction of elsewhere.

As we walk, and I'm struggling by this point to keep up, Ray is talking.

"Do you remember the first time we came here?" he says, while we're still in the cemetery.

"Sure." I say. "The night of Sam's house party, yeah?"

"Yeah. That was the first time I met you, you know."

"Was it?" I say, an edge that I'm not proud of to my voice.

"Don't worry… this isn't some weird unrequited love from beyond the grave thing." He laughs. "It's just a coincidence that it was that night."

"Oh, right. So, yeah, we were all a bit drunk, and a couple of us were on acid, and… there were a few of us, yeah."

"Nearly a dozen. None of the girls were out stomping, 'cos they were knackered and it was freezing, but we decided that we were going to go on an adventure."

"We were… what were we doing? You had a Dictaphone, and…"

The thing about acid is it's a clarifying drug, and you shouldn't ever let anyone tell you otherwise. At least, as weird as things might get, I always found that I'd retain clarity throughout. Every now and then Tanya and I will have a couple of glasses of wine each with dinner, and I'd be hard pressed to give you many details of those nights now; everything quickly becomes a sleepy blur. But Ray invokes that one night and suddenly I'm back in that moment, nearly three decades before, remembering sensations and sounds, and what the hell we were doing there in the first place.

"…That Dictaphone had been doing the rounds all night. One of the girls was doing a tape for Big Yellow Matty, because he was stationed out in Cyprus or somewhere. Someone decided they wanted to see the sunrise, and then suddenly there were a dozen of us, and *you* decided that we should record the dawn for Matty."

"Which in retrospect sounds a bit fucking stupid." says Ray.

"Mm." I say.

"Get a shift on, then, mate." he says.

We're heading for the highest point within walking distance, which happens to be a field on the western edge of town. All those years ago we were cutting it fine, and now we're cutting it fine again now. We walk in silence for a while, concentrating on speed. We're using shortcuts that I haven't used since that night, but Ray remembers them all. We stomp through a part of the town centre that I'm not convinced we're allowed to go through - there are gates and everything - and we beat the pavement in as near as dammit a straight line toward the sun.

The sky is getting lighter when we hit the edge of concrete at the town's boundaries, and it's obvious that we're going to make it, just.

The field is on a hill. Not much more than a mound really, but I remember clearly the impression that it wasn't a hill but the curve of the earth that we were traversing. And today it feels the same. We walk across the field, dodging cow shit, and as the ground slopes underneath us it feels as if we aren't moving forward at all. We're walking on the spot, the planet moving under us as we go, and as the incline grows the illusion deepens, and the world isn't moving under us. We're pushing it round.

And when we hit the highest point and stop it's like being in a fast car and hitting the brakes. The world takes longer to slow down than we do, and I rock on my heels. I glance over at Ray, who grins back. We both turn and look to the horizon. A slice of the sun makes an appearance and I remember that the last time it felt almost audible, like a choral ringing in my ears.

That doesn't happen this time but it's exciting all the same. But sunrise is always faster than you think it'll be, isn't it? As we stand and watch it goes from a slither to a lozenge to an egg yolk, and then it bubbles up, a last few seconds of comfort against the solid black line of the horizon before bursting upward, finally a perfect circle.

I look back down the hill. The town swings and sweeps around behind us, parts of it still in shadow, and all still wreathed in mist.

Ray speaks.

"Something major is happening, and I don't really know what comes next." he says. "But I figured my parents will probably still be there in a bit, and the one thing I realised I really wanted to do when I got back was this. And it wouldn't have been quite the same on my own."

I look across at him. In direct sunlight the moisture at his skin is calmer than it was by the light of the moon, and I consider for the first time that he had held the phone, and worn the earphones, and I don't know what might be left of a man who'd been in the ground for such a long time, and what they might be made of now. Very thin tendrils of steam are coming off his cheeks, coiling up only to fall back to his head moments later.

"Oh." I say, which seems pretty inadequate on the face of it.

"There haven't been many sunrises these last few years, is the thing." he says, and I nod, because to be honest I can relate. The dead don't have the time, and the living don't find it.

We stand and watch the sun, and wait for the next thing to happen.

Maybe...

You had only been back in the hotel room twenty minutes before the noises started.

At first it was just a single loud voice. Probably a man on the phone, or one side of a one-sided conversation in the room next door.

Then, the more muffled sounds of voices lowered to a murmur. Two people, it sounded like, but hard to tell if the second voice was male or female.

A short, reedy moan, and then a gentle thump, like someone just sat on a bed that is up against the shared wall. Then the rhythmic sound of the headboard rocking against it.

Maybe you found it funny at first. Or maybe you're in that room with your wife or husband or lover, and the thought of lust in the next room excited you both for a while.

But then the sound built, joined with less familiar human sounds, more pain than pleasure, and maybe you realised that what was happening next door wasn't what you had first thought. Or maybe your companion started getting impatient with your unseen neighbours. Or you were sitting there alone, and getting lonely, and desperate.

Whatever the case, at some point you decided to bang on the shared wall in protest, and that decision turned to action.

And the noises stopped.

You probably assumed that you'd made your point. That the people in the next room realised, embarrassed, that they were loud enough to be heard. That they were lying there, naked under the covers, exchanging furtive glances, suitably cowed. Or silent, and spent.

Or maybe the sudden quiet makes you nervous. Maybe you're paranoid; have an over-active imagination.

Maybe you're picturing me or someone like me, standing here still, staring at the other side of the wall. Trying to work out where exactly your head might be on the other side of that thin layer of plaster.

Maybe not. Probably too much of an outlier; too unlikely a scenario for you to imagine.

Too much of a coincidence that I could have finished the work I came here to do at the exact same moment your patience ran out.

I tidy up the tools of my trade, and look over at the shared wall again. I think momentarily on the order in the world, and the chaos. The terrible things that can drop into your life without any warning. A shiver goes through me. It isn't unpleasant.

I check my watch, and do some quick calculations with the numbers it shows me. No rush.

Maybe you shouldn't have put yourself on my radar.

Printed in Great Britain
by Amazon